Peter Michael Rosenberg is a young British author with outstanding talent. His first novel, *Kissing through a Pane of Glass*, was the runner up in the 1992 Betty Trask Prize and Awards and on publication it received widespread critical acclaim. His third novel, *Because It Makes My Heart Beat Faster*, is now available.

Peter Michael Rosenberg lives in North London. He is currently at work on his fourth novel.

Also by Peter Michael Rosenberg

Kissing through a Pane of Glass
Because It Makes My Heart Beat Faster

Touched by a God or Something

Peter Michael Rosenberg

TOUCHSTONE BOOKS
LONDON . NEW YORK . SYDNEY . TOKYO . TORONTO . SINGAPORE

First published in Great Britain by Simon & Schuster Ltd, 1994
First published in Touchstone, 1995
An imprint of Simon & Schuster Ltd
A Paramount Communications Company

Simon & Schuster Ltd
West Garden Place
Kendal Street
London W2 2AQ

Simon & Schuster of Australia Pty Ltd
Sydney

A CIP catalogue record for this book is available from the British Library.

ISBN 0-671-85093-8

Printed and bound in Great Britain by
HarperCollins Manufacturing, Glasgow

For Sara

Acknowledgements

My heartfelt thanks go to Lucy Ferguson for her editing skills and encouragement, and to Christopher Little, my agent, for his continuing support and determined efforts on my behalf. Thanks too to David Greschler, whose interest helped nurture the seed of this novel so many years ago.

1

The smell is everything. It is the constant, ever-present trigger that reminds me I am here, not there; that I am elsewhere. Last night, exhausted beyond reason, I took the precaution of wrapping a pillow – this feather-pillow, musty and fibrous – tightly about my head to muffle any intrusive sounds. But I wasn't counting on the strange smells; I wasn't expecting odours to penetrate these makeshift defences and announce their presence with such incontrovertible assurance. It hadn't occurred to me that something as innocent as a smell would cause such distress.

Not that it was an unpleasant smell – nothing fetid, putrid or decomposing. Nothing . . . *human*. Just the rare perfume of pine needles, dry and crisp, wafting in from the patio. The fragrance of this other world, my new world, as natural, as *essential* a component of this air as oxygen, yet totally alien to me. Not a London smell, no; not a London smell at all.

Breathe it in; breathe it in, deeply. Would you have recognised it out of context and identified its source? It is no simple odour – a balanced fragrance, floating gently in the air like a feather on the breeze. It has a richness and complexity borne of natural ingredients, like that which you'd find in, say, ground roasted coffee beans or freshly squeezed oranges, its components inter-mingled in perfect proportions. You could not manufacture it accurately from its individual parts and achieve, with any accuracy, that subtle blend of highs and lows, of deep bass notes and treble trills. You could not reproduce it synthetically. It is both special and strange.

I have a theory about this richly pungent and evocative odour. One day, when I least expect it, this smell, this very particular smell, will return unannounced. Bypassing all other senses, creeping effortlessly past the censors and sneaking under every safe-guard with the proficiency of a skilled limbo dancer, it will hurl me back, à la Proust, to this moment, to these memories, to this place.

Yet one more thing to dread.

Sniff. I am here.

'Go,' said Cassandra.

The word resounded in my ears as I woke, body numb, a hint of daylight dancing behind closed blinds. I shifted slightly, gazed at the unfamiliar ceiling, the anonymous walls, grasping for recognition in those short-lived, desolate moments that lie trapped between sound-asleep and wide-awake. Amazing, even now, even after everything, how terrifying, how unequiv-ocally shit-scaring, bollock-numbingly frightening those moments can be . . . the closest we ever come to being totally, utterly lost. Really. Take it from me. Take it from someone who knows.

It was dark in the room, too dark to identify the outlines of the strange, amorphous entities that sur-rounded me, perching tentatively on shelves, hanging ominously from the ceiling, crouching suspiciously on the floor. It took a great effort of will, muddle-headed and dry-throated as I was, to convince myself that I was not about to be attacked: clubbed to death by a pile of clothes, knifed in the back by a table lamp. Stupid, I know. But no less frightening for all that.

It took an even greater effort to lever myself off the bed and onto my feet. My body felt immobilised, as if someone had tampered with my starter-motor and filled my chassis full of lead. I felt weary and exhausted, weighed down by my conscience, my evil deeds. Or something worse; the collected wrong-doings of my ancestors, perhaps, or original sin.

Or maybe it was just jetlag.

Achieving the perpendicular with the sort of graceless exertions usually reserved for new-born foals and dangerous drunks, I stumbled to the window and pulled the curtain to one side. Wisps of light filtered through the olive-wood slats. Winter morning light – cool, Mediterranean – threw the room and its contents into sharp relief. Exposed, the table lamp skulked into the corner; the pile of clothes cowered beneath my glare. That haunting, unmistakable fragrance seeped in through the spaces in between. Cicadas resonated outside: a foreign music.

I stood there silently for a moment or two, trying to assimilate my new surroundings, to come to terms with my new environment. But I did not succeed.

I must have stayed awake until three, maybe four in the morning following that terrible flight, my mind alert, tuned in to Radio England, to London, eagerly picking up the frequencies of home. Buzz. I could not turn it off, I could not shut it out. Buzz buzz. Stray thoughts, idle concerns, real fears; all strung together in a meaningless, irritating jumble, a spider's web of worry. Mind buzzing,

I call it; like an itch you can't scratch. Buzz buzz buzz. I hate it. Really, it drives me mad. What are you supposed to do when your own brain does that to you? I mean, who's in charge here? No wonder I'm exhausted. First the panic, then the plane journey, then, when I'm expending every last effort to keep my shit together, my brain goes pfoof!, and my mind turns on me. Fuck it, as if I haven't got enough things to worry about. Is it any wonder I look the way I do?

'Go,' she said. 'Go and don't come back.' That's what she said. There was no kindness in her tone, no concern. Just that terrible, terrible desperation. It was not a request; it was an order. I must do my duty. I must do the right thing.

But what is the right thing? She didn't tell me. She simply didn't say.

Cassandra's expressions devoured grown men at a hundred paces. Cassandra's sneer scorched flesh. Cassandra's voice made time stand still. I am here, not because I wish it, but because Cassandra said so.

'Go,' said Cassandra. So I went.

I've no idea what I'm going to do, now that I'm here. Not in a place like this. What was I thinking? Ah yes, I remember now ... I wasn't thinking. I was reacting. Like the aeroplane that brought me here, I was on auto-pilot. I was doing what I had been programmed to do. And now I'm here, I must fulfil those prearranged instructions. But there's no hurry. These are early days; there's plenty of time. There is, in fact, no limit to the time I must spend in this retreat.

'Go,' said Cassandra, 'and don't come back until ...'

Until what? Until I'm better? Is that what you had intended to say, Cassandra? And if so, better than what?

But Cassandra never finished the sentence. She just gave me that look; that look that I'll never forget. A look that, no matter what else happens, will never be erased from my mind. Consequently, I may not return *until*. These are my instructions; I am here, *until*.

It's a little vague, don't you think?

And how will I occupy my time? Travelling? Soul-searching? A little psychological self-examination? Or just endless emotional self-flagellation?

Not that Cassandra cares any more, but that's another matter.

There is a great deal to tell, so much to explain. And it appears, despite myself, despite my exhaustion and confusion, that I must start telling you now. A confession, I suppose. I had hoped I might lure you in seductively, as Cassandra lured me. I wanted to tease you. But I cannot. I must speak. I *must* speak.

So let me start by telling you about Cassandra. Let me tell you everything about the woman who banished me to these foreign lands.

She was . . . she was . . . oh God, where to start? I want to say 'Cassandra was extraordinary', but I know you'll just smirk. Real people, real flesh and blood people are rarely extraordinary, and when a man says this about a woman it usually means just one thing: infatuation. But I am not, nor was I ever, infatuated with Cassandra. Infatuation is a feather, a lightweight, barely substantial thing that can be blown away in a breeze. There was never anything lightweight about Cassandra, nor her effect upon me (or anyone else, for that matter). So how do we go about this unenviable task of describing Cassandra? With paradox? Hyperbole? It will, I fear, all sound vaguely ridiculous, another characteristic that could not, with accuracy, ever be applied to Cassandra herself.

Take a breath. A deep breath. Here we go.

Cassandra was tall for her height; I kid you not. Cassandra carried herself with the poise of a princess, the stealth of a leopard. It was a source of constant amazement that someone of a mere five feet six inches could tower over others who possessed a two-, three- or even six-inch advantage. But that was Cassandra. Cassandra walked into a crowded room and the assembled parted like the waters of the Red Sea before Moses. Cassandra shimmered along a busy high street and the multitudes stopped in their tracks, turned and stared. Cassandra wandered to the front of a long queue and people stepped aside to let her through. Not because she was unduly physical, nor because she was uniquely beautiful, but simply because of a total and almost overwhelming self-assurance that brooked no uncertainties, conceded no flaws. People deferred to Cassandra naturally, as if it were a reflex, no more questionable than blinking or scratching. And she accepted this as if it were her right, her entitlement.

Cassandra's beauty was anachronistic, setting her apart from the crowds of would-be models or aspiring film stars. It singled her out for special attention. She was not pretty in contemporary terms, and yet you could not help but admire her good looks, which were robust and guaranteed to make you think: 'where have I seen her before?' Inevitably, you would have been reminded of the golden age of Hollywood, or perhaps eras of even greater distinction. You would have admired her vaguely oriental eyes, her slightly snub nose, her full and perfectly seductive lips. You would have wished to run your fingers through her straight, jet black hair, or stroke the curve of her neck. Should you have been fortunate enough to have been introduced to her at, say, a cocktail party, her appearance was so striking that you would probably have forgotten her name and embarrassed yourself by calling her Cleopatra. You think this absurd? I saw it happen. Twice.

Ah, Cassandra; she walked the earth like she'd been touched by a God or something. Which was good news for Cassandra, but made life pretty tough on mere mortals like you and me.

But perhaps you're still not convinced. After all, there are many beautiful, charismatic, powerful women in the world; why should this one be of special interest? All I can say is: she was not like other women. She was nothing like other women, and if you stay with me long enough, you will discover the truth about Cassandra for yourself.

But this is all too much, too fast . . . I must slow down. I must pace myself. This isn't an easy story to listen to, and it certainly isn't an easy one to tell. But the good things in life, they're not easy, are they.

Are they?

Did I mention her clothes? Did I explain that Cassandra could don sack-cloth and ashes and still look as desirable and as delectable as something that has just stepped out of the pages of *Vogue*? Even when lounging around the house in jeans and t-shirt she gave the appearance of having been dressed by experts especially for the occasion. What was it about Cassandra that gave her this ability to look so . . . *exceptional*? Let us discover this elusive essence, reproduce it, bottle it, sell it to the masses and make our fame and fortune.

Forgive me this indulgence. I know what you must be

thinking, but it isn't as simple as that. Nothing concerning Cassandra was ever simple.

The sun looks fierce yet somehow comforting. When I left London it was shrouded in that damp, stultifying cloud that seems to hang around all winter like an unwanted house-guest who has outstayed his welcome, always promising to move on, but somehow never quite getting around to it. At least I'll be free of that for a while. For ever, perhaps.

I shall probably take a stroll later on and check out my surroundings. After all, I really have no idea where I am. I arrived in darkness, and allowed myself to be led by some unsavoury tout who spoke just enough English to convince me he was both unreliable and untrustworthy. But what alternatives were there? I just had to take his word that the 'apartment', as he called it, would be close to the centre of town.

I have to be close to the centre, to the hustle and bustle, to the crowds of strangers. I can't afford to be isolated, separate. I need to be one of many, unexceptional, invisible. I shall be here for some time, that much is certain. There is nowhere else for me to go. Not just for the moment.

I don't know about this – this place, that is. But when you're in a hurry you have to take what you can get, and the first available flight was heading east, I didn't require a visa, so . . .

It's extraordinary what we do, don't you think? I mean, just turning up at an airport and jumping on the first plane heading somewhere, anywhere. Not the sort of thing I would have done under normal circumstances, of course, but no less exciting for all that. And never had time seemed so precious, so rare a commodity. I expended so little of it packing a bag and running to the station you'd have thought I only had an hour's worth of life left to me. And at Gatwick, jumping off the train, running up the escalator at the airport, buying a ticket, zipping through passport control and dashing to the plane – like a man with a mission. Like a man possessed. Not even enough time to visit the duty free. Not that it was exactly uppermost in my mind. Still, a bottle of Scotch wouldn't have gone amiss. I might have slept better.

And I wasn't afraid. Not at all. I'm not afraid of flying; I'm not scared of strange, foreign countries. Although, frankly, I could have done with a bit more money. But Cassandra didn't keep much cash in the house, so I'll have to make do with the three hundred pounds she had thoughtfully withdrawn for me, plus all I had in my wallet. It'll have to do for now. It's not much, but if the taxi ride from the airport was anything to go by, the cost of living here is cheap, so I'll survive.

Let's face it; what choice do I have?

2

Our lives are mapped out in conversations.

First conversation:

She slid across the room as if she were on roller skates. She was wearing a short, black, sleeveless dress, black tights, heavy eye make-up and a sneer. I thought she was ravishing. I had been watching her all evening; it was the only thing worth doing. I hated parties, and had only turned up because it was Jenny's thirtieth birthday and she said I was turning into a scruffy, antisocial hermit. Still, I hardly knew anyone there and those that I recognised seemed intent on avoiding me. I think I must have been giving off my 'leave me alone' vibes. When you've been cooped up inside one room for weeks on end with nothing but a typewriter and Radio Four for company, you do tend to get a bit stand-offish.

Anyway, there I was, minding my own business, nursing a drink and ogling every biped that looked vaguely female, when this vision set her sights on me from the other side of the room, and then homed in on me like a heat-seeking missile. I didn't even have time to check my armpits for unsightly damp patches. Before I knew it, she was standing directly in front of me, peering straight into my eyes. It was the boldest, coldest come-on I'd ever encountered. An Australian friend once told me that, at night in the outback, a kangaroo caught in the glare of the headlights of an oncoming vehicle becomes temporarily paralysed by the bright lights. It just seizes up. And invariably, it gets run over.

As for that first conversation, it went something like this:

'Do you want to dance?'

'Err . . .'

' "Er?" Oh dear. I mean, it's hardly a difficult question,' she said, and then eyed me up and down rather deliberately. 'You remember dancing, don't you? You wiggle your hips and prance around like a flat-footed fairy during the fast numbers, and then wait impatiently for the slow one so you can paw me and dribble in my ear.' She smiled, not very pleasantly. My stomach turned.

'In which case, no thanks.' I blushed and walked across the room through the epileptic frenzy of party-goers and sought solace in the kitchen with a bottle of Scotch. A strange, beautiful woman had just seen fit to make a complete fool of me, and I had no idea why.

When I asked Jenny about her, she just shrugged and said something about 'friend of a friend'. For some reason, the fact that Jenny didn't know her comforted me. I remember feeling oddly mischievous.

Second conversation:

'Do you want to fuck?'

'What?'

' "What?" ' I mimicked, making my best effort to focus on her. An hour had passed, during which time the mystery woman had avoided me. I had managed, however, to consume half a bottle of whisky, which had

11

not only loosened my tongue, but had also instilled in me a very false and quite uncharacteristic recklessness. I had sidled up to her whilst she was helping herself to a glass of punch.

'It isn't very complicated,' I said. Now it was her turn to be embarrassed. I let the alcohol talk for me. 'You remember fucking, don't you? You open your legs and pretend that you're desirable, fake an orgasm while waiting impatiently for me to come, then hope to God I don't tell you you're a lousy lay.'

There. That did it, I thought. But of course, I didn't know Cassandra then, did I?

She glared at me for some considerable time, then smiled.

'Your place or mine?' she said.

Third conversation:
    'You were too quick . . . '
    'Oh for Christsake!'
    'You were.'
    'I'm not a machine . . . '
    'You mean you're not as good as a machine.'
    'Go fuck yourself!'
    'Go to hell!'
    And I didn't even know her name.

Not an especially auspicious start, I'll admit. I don't even recall clearly how we ended up in bed together, but I *can* tell you that it was her place, not mine. That was how it would always be. What I do remember with greater clarity is how Cassandra, not content to shock me with her unambiguous verbal invitation, took the opportunity to add a physical dimension to my bewilderment. Cassandra, I would soon learn, was very good

12

at that: the pre-emptive strike followed swiftly by the devastating bombshell. In this instance, having disarmed me with her casually calculated 'your place or mine', which almost made me swallow my own tongue, she then grabbed me, firmly but gently, by the balls. It was to be the first and last time that Cassandra ever treated me with anything approaching tenderness.

It is a simple law of physics (or biology . . . or maybe metaphysics) that, if you happen to be a man, where the balls go, the rest of the body follows. A fact with which Cassandra, who happens to be a woman, was none the less *au fait*. Within minutes I was being strapped into the front seat of her gleaming white Golf GTi, and the next thing I knew we were racing westwards through the night. We spoke not a word.

Cassandra slammed a cassette into the stereo and the loud, bass-heavy opening riff of Bruce Springsteen's 'Born to Run' thundered out of every corner of the car. It was like being inside a speeding ghetto-blaster. It seemed an odd choice of music, both anachronistic and geographically irrelevant. As far as I was concerned, 'Born to Run' was a golden oldie; one of those classic mid-seventies rock anthems that roused and inspired a generation of teenagers who were too young to have remembered James Dean, but still wanted to believe in the great American myth of the rebel outsider and the open road. A bit bombastic, touchingly naïve, but not a bad song for all that. At least, that's what it meant to me, looking back from an altogether more cynical, less idealistic era. But I could sense that it meant something very different to Cassandra. She was so familiar with the song, mouthing the lyrics and grinning wildly, that I soon realised that this was no unsophisticated, idealistic rant to her. This was a part of her life, part of her youth; perhaps, in fact, the anthem of the gawky, adolescent Cassandra, all innocence and ignorance, hungry for freedom and dreaming of escape.

At the time, of course, with the music booming around me, I was neither this precise nor as lucid in my evaluation of the song and its ramifications *vis à vis* the complete stranger sitting beside me. I was too busy concentrating on keeping the remains of the half bottle of Scotch inside me, particularly as we raced through the tree-lined chicanes of north London. But one thing was certain. The track dated her. If Cassandra had grown up with this music then she was now in her early thirties.

An older woman.

We had only been in the car a few minutes, or so it seemed, when we suddenly screeched to a halt and I found myself being bundled unceremoniously out of the car, up some steep stone steps and through a doorway into a darkened hallway.

I was still feeling a bit shaky from the booze and would have liked a moment or two to accustom myself to my new surroundings. But Cassandra did not waste time by turning on the lights or putting on the kettle or even asking me to make myself at home. She simply dragged me into the front room, pulled me to the floor and began tugging my clothes off. The curtains were wide open, allowing the eerily fused illumination of full moon and sodium-vapour streetlamp to flood in through the huge bay window. The light, ghostly and fluorescent, seemed to shift and shimmer, especially in the more hidden recesses of the room. It felt as if the place were full of sprites and spectres, a not altogether pleasant sensation.

Not that I had much time to think about this. Cassandra had fallen upon me with such suddenness, such

14

verve and gusto, that I was too surprised to protest. And it wasn't that I objected to the substance of the event, just – how should I put it – the tone. Whilst this wasn't exactly a rape, she had not actually sought my consent. Even as I felt my underpants being whisked off and Cassandra's warm exhalation – the breath of life – bringing me to attention, I was aware that things were progressing with perhaps undue haste. Which may well account for Cassandra's subsequent disappointment and the stream of invective that she hurled at me following our less than resplendent coupling.

She did, of course, insist that she drive me home.

I cannot say for certain why I agreed to see her again. It was her idea – she suggested it at four that morning as she was shoving me onto the kerb – and I never bothered to question it. The fact is, I hadn't had a girlfriend for the best part of a year, or more pertinently, I hadn't had sex. This wasn't simply a case of bad luck: it was part of a plan. It just so happened that, a few days after I had concluded that this particular plan had run its course, Cassandra waltzed into my world.

So, why would any normal, healthy man make a deliberate choice to eschew sexual contact with women for a year? Well, it's all because of the writing.

My decision to become a full-time writer at the ripe old age of twenty-four and give up regular, paid employment, swiftly proved to be the financial equivalent of walking a tightrope without a net. I had already toyed with the idea of being a writer for a couple of years, and had seduced myself with visions of being a famous novelist. However, I had discovered at an early juncture that I was, to all intents and purposes, a thoroughly lazy

15

bastard, and that writing, for all its pretensions and potential pleasures, was just another form of hard work. As these two notions (idleness and industry) were at odds, I had to find a way of disciplining myself for the rigorous task of sitting down daily in front of a blank piece of paper and *creating*.

During the first few weeks of my new vocation, I read everything I could on the act of creation, hoping to discover an easy way of ensuring that writing became a pleasurable necessity rather than an unenviable task. Writers' autobiographies were at the top of the list and I consumed these at a rate of knots. Tomes with rather forbidding titles like *Creativity and Power: the Politics of Artistic Expression* and *Bring Into Being: Creativity and the Reproductive Urge* were further grist to the mill. I even researched literary magazines for interviews with novelists going back through the ages, intent on uncovering the secret formulae that kept them going. I longed for stories of revelation through writing, of tapping great mysteries through contemplation, of achieving incomparable fulfilment through invention.

What I learnt, much to my chagrin, was that whilst all these goals may have been achievable on a practical level, without doubt the greatest incentive to continue writing day in day out was assuaging hunger. I wanted to give up the part-time and casual work that prevented me from writing full-time. But I knew that, as a writer, if you didn't write, you didn't sell, and if you didn't sell, you didn't eat/drink/live. As banal as this was, it soon proved to be an irrefutable truism. Besides, I really did want to produce something worthwhile. I could think of nothing more satisfying than reading a favourable review in the *Sunday Times* of, say, my first novel. A review replete with sufficient superlatives to satisfy even

16

the most needy and insecure writer. But it wasn't going to happen if I did not – as some deeply prosaic author wrote – apply the seat of my pants to the seat of my chair.

That took care of motivation. Now there was the simple matter of application. Whilst I do not subscribe to the school of thought that considers it necessary to suffer in order to write, there is no doubt in my mind that if you are perfectly content with life as it stands, you're quite simply *never* going to produce great art. If you're living in the lap of luxury, eating Châteaubriand, drinking fine Napoleon brandy and getting regular, rampant sex on demand, lets face it, why should you give a shit about producing anything more work-intensive than a great, smug, self-satisfied smile? Precisely.

At this time I was living in a gruesome bedsit in North London, a place that afforded me all the luxury of a personalised cesspit. Experience had already shown me that, even if I hadn't eaten a decent meal in weeks and the notion of comfort had become just a distant memory, if there was a woman around, my productivity took a nose dive. It didn't matter how hungry I was for success, how desperate for recognition, how intent on completing my work. If there was a choice between sitting in front of a typewriter and staring at a blank piece of paper until my brain started dribbling from my ears, or snuggling up under the duvet with a gorgeous, cuddly and erotically oriented sex-kitten, then there was no contest. Honeypot had it over inkwell every time.

Clearly, this caused me no little anxiety. For a while I believed that writing and regular sexual activity were not only incompatible, but antithetical. That my creative energy (as I visualised it) was regulated, like petrol flowing from a pump, and that it could be channelled in one way or another. But that ultimately there was only so much of it to burn, and that if I was busy banging I would be incapable of writing anything more taxing than my signature. One thing was certain. On the occasions when I became involved with a woman, even if it was only for a few days, my writing suffered. As I was determined to hit the big-time, to have both the critically acclaimed Meisterwerk and the huge international bestseller, after two years of getting nowhere I made a resolute decision to become a full-time writer. And in order to maximise my chances of success, I would eschew all sexual activity for one full year.

Such decisions are not made lightly, and considering that I was still in my twenties and therefore at my sexual peak, I felt I was making the greatest sacrifice of all: laying down my sex life for my art. It felt like a grand and noble gesture; all great artists had had to make sacrifices in the past, so it made perfect sense that I too should pay homage to my own creativity with this renunciation. I would be celibate for a twelve-month period, and see if it made any difference.

It did. I was still lazy, I was still penniless, and I still lived like a complete slob, only now I also had to contend with the sort of terminal sexual frustration that might beset a trussed up rabbit. The result, perhaps inevitably, was creative constipation on a grand scale. It was as if every exit had been barricaded, every orifice boarded up. Whilst other writers were artistically challenged, I was creatively clogged. If other authors were imaginatively disadvantaged, I was productively choked. Where other scribes were blocked, I was plugged, bunged and stoppered.

And this is how it continued for the best part of a year. It seems ludicrous that I should have continued with this exercise when it was so clearly working against me, but I felt I had to see the venture through to the end or else admit failure.

Thus it was that, shortly before that fateful party, I had decided to bring my experiment with self-imposed abstinence to an end. That I might have to continue celibate for some time thereafter did not, at the time, concern me. By this stage my sexual fantasies were so detailed and profound that I felt certain I could create a sexual partner from out of the ether, just by willing it. In keeping with the ritualised procedures that had brought me to this crisis, I set myself a date, after which I could allow myself to plunge again into the pleasures of the flesh.

Once released from my vows, I spent several nights just hanging around my local pub, eyeing up the native talent and trying to remember a few decent chat-up lines. I felt strangely out of my depth and vaguely traumatised by my long self-denial, like a crash victim who has to get in a car and learn to drive again. After about four days of this, I received a phone call from Jenny, inviting me to her thirtieth birthday party. She assured me there would be plenty of unattached women in attendance.

As you now know, I attended the party and spent the whole evening anticipating the thrills of the chase once more: eyes meeting across the room, first acknowledgement, first touch, first kiss, first grope; the night concluding with a bout of wonderful, wild, celebratory sex with a passionate, carnally obsessed nymphet who was willing to subjugate her will to my desire and fulfil my every fantasy.

And what I got was Cassandra, telling me that, when

it came to sex, I was less impressive than a piece of injection moulded polypropelene with a six-volt motor inserted in one end.

You'd think, perhaps, that this would be enough to have me running for the hills. However, one must not forget that when Cassandra came along, I was like someone who had been on a strict, self-imposed diet for a year. Such people are likely to have become so emaciated that their reasoning has been severely affected. I was, in a manner of speaking, starving to death. So when this indubitably sexy woman approached me at a party and started throwing these come-ons at me, and then followed it up by whisking me off to her home with the express intention of having her way with me, what could I do but rise to the bait?

Not that I was interested in anything serious. Far from it. As Kev, my best mate, would have said – it was just a bit of a laugh. Although frankly, in all the time I knew Cassandra, there was never so much as a giggle shared. But that's neither here nor there.

For my part, Cassandra was a good-looking woman with a terrific body who had as much warmth as a packet of frozen vegetables, and an inexhaustible line in insults, put-downs and curses which were sometimes amusing, often disturbing but always effective. Yet despite her sharp tongue and total candour, I found myself drawn to her – or rather, to her bed – time and again. Why I was prepared to suffer the indignities of being labelled 'limp dick', 'pitiful wimp' and 'hopeless wanker' is still something of a mystery to me. I'd never previously allowed anyone to insult me so regularly and with such malice. Why Cassandra should have put up with my curses of 'foul-mouthed whore', 'callous bitch' and 'frozen fucking fish' is equally perplexing. None the less, during the days and weeks that followed, our relationship flourished, based wholly, I believe, on mutual disgust.

Ah, here they are; here are the pine needles, dry and crisp on the stone patio, releasing their pungent odour like little bottles of spilt perfume. At least no one can look in on me here; I need to have my privacy, more now than ever. This will be a pleasant spot in which to relax during the late afternoon and watch the sun go down over the distant hills. If I can relax, that is. Perhaps I should buy some Scotch, if they sell it here. A drink on the patio in the late afternoon sun . . . yes, that should help.

I wonder what my neighbours do? I wonder how inquisitive they are? Are they used to seeing a foreigner wandering in and out of this apartment block? Maybe these rooms are all for tourists, for visitors. I hope nobody around here speaks English. I don't want to talk to anyone just now; I don't want to say a thing. I want my space, understand? I want to be alone.

I just . . . I just *have* to be left alone.

3

Cassandra and I knew little about each other's lives in that first month. Her profession, her upbringing, her history – all these things were of no consequence to me. I did not *want* to know anything about her. Not because I was not curious; I knew that curiosity – about people, places, life, everything – was a prerequisite for an author. No, I did not want to know details because I did not want to get involved. I realised very early on that here was an opportunity to enjoy the perfect relationship, a liaison in which I could benefit from all of the pleasures (sex, oneupmanship, degradation) and suffer none of the drawbacks (emotional intimacy, caring, commitment). A relationship devoid of pretence, dishonesty, responsibility and, most of all, love. If I played this right, I knew Cassandra could be the perfect partner.

And it seemed to be a mutually satisfactory arrangement. Cassandra rarely enquired about my line of work, my emotional or physical health or what I was thinking at any time, and I offered little unsolicited information. We communicated almost solely via tactile investigations and derogatory (and frequently inappropriate) comments.

It must be said that I had never met anyone quite like

Cassandra before. Neither had I ever entered into so blatantly sexual a relationship, one in which not a glimmer of affection existed. We did not hate each other – hate is far too strong an expression, and suggests a certain emotional interaction between two parties. We meant far too little to each other at that stage to entertain anything other than this constant, vindictive disdain, with an undercurrent of mild, suppressed violence. Not physical violence, of course; we never hit, kicked or struck each other in any way (although Cassandra did once, in the heat of passion, deliver a bite of such precision to my upper arm as to cause a thin line of blood to seep through the skin in an almost perfect ellipse). All in all, it was a bit like playing a not very good game, when the only alternative is not to play at all.

I told no one about Cassandra; I didn't feel that this was, as yet, a lasting or even vaguely stable arrangement and consequently there seemed no reason to advertise the fact that I was seeing someone. At least, this is how I justified it to myself. More probably, I was just a bit embarrassed about having to explain or defend a liaison which seemed to have no virtue, and no pleasant or explicable reason for existing. I wasn't in love, it wasn't anything serious, and I could think of no one with whom I wished to share the information that I, a struggling pauper, was sleeping with an upper-class harpy called, for Godsake, Cassandra Beauchamp, for no other reason, it seemed, than sexual relief. See what I mean? No matter how you looked at it, it sounded sordid.

And there was no likelihood of any of my friends finding out about her by accident. As far as I could tell she had virtually gate-crashed Jenny's party, and so it was assured that we had no one in common. We were never seen out together (our affair, at this time, was limited strictly to our twice-weekly night-time trysts at Cassandra's rather comfortable house in Hampstead) and as I lived alone in my tawdry Turnpike Lane bedsit, there was no one to enquire as to why my bedsheets were left unruffled on so many occasions.

The rest of the time, when I wasn't servicing Cassandra, I continued to live as I had done for the previous year. I would spend a statutory eight hours a day at the type-writer. I knew by that stage that I had to employ the disciplines imposed by a timetable or else I was prone to lie around in bed all day reading other people's master-pieces and getting depressed.

The regime I drafted seemed to fulfil all the necessary requirements, apportioning sufficient time for work and sleep, whilst still managing to accommodate what I though of as 'survival duties'.

As I worked best at night I would usually find myself rising at about noon. I'd throw on some clothes and stroll to the corner shop for a pint of milk and the *Guardian*, which I studied over a leisurely breakfast. (I had to think of it as 'study'; reading was something you did for pleasure, in one's leisure hours, and I was far too 'busy', much too 'committed' to have anything as luxurious as leisure time.)

By one o'clock, I'd have brought myself up to date on current affairs and the latest movements in the business world, and have familiarised myself with recent reviews of artistic events that I could afford neither the time nor money to see. I was then ready to deal with the daily business of cleaning the flat, shopping, washing clothes, et cetera. By three I'd be at my desk, staring at the typewriter, mind relaxed, eyes sparkling, back straight,

24

fingers poised over the keyboard, looking for all the world like an especially perky puppy, begging for a bone.

These afternoon sessions were usually set aside for re-reading and re-writing any new material from the previous night's session. Of all the habits I developed during this time, this was probably the most useful as far as my authorial life was concerned. I was always amazed to discover, in the cold, clear light of day, that the golden prose that had poured out of me like a gushing geyser during the darkened hours was, in fact, unadulterated tripe; less a golden geyser than a stagnant pond, full of murky, rotting refuse.

Salvaging the rare gem from this pile of garbage (or, as Kev would say, sifting the shit from the sugar) would consume most of the afternoon. Any spare time was utilised trying to diminish the ever growing (and increasingly dangerous) pile of unanswered correspondence that accumulated beside the desk, and which threatened to avalanche at any time and bury me in three feet of exotic 'wish you were here' postcards and final demands.

I'd break to catch the six o'clock news, make myself something to eat, watch something mindless on the box, and by ten I'd be ready for the big surge. I would sit at that desk from ten until four in the morning, breast-beating and soul-searching, ever hopeful that, at some time during those six mystical hours, I would turn out something magnificent, something wonderful, something unique . . . or just something that would not have to be despatched to the wastepaper bin the following afternoon.

Regardless of whether or not these supposedly creative periods were successful, there was always something magical about these night-time sessions. I loved writing at that late hour, when most of the rest of the world had gone to sleep, leaving me alone to concentrate on my art. In summer I would open the windows wide and allow the night sounds of the city to sneak into the room. A single anglepoise cast its yellowing tungsten light over the typewriter, and threw huge, industrious shadows onto the wall beside me. I'd tune the radio into some late night music programme – usually a pirate jazz or soul station – and have it turned up just loud enough to form an aural backdrop that seeped into my consciousness but did not distract me from my work. I'd stay awake with numerous cups of coffee and an endless supply of cigarettes, and would sometimes lose myself in the wisps and curls of light-grey smoke as they spiralled up into the shade of the anglepoise lamp.

There was something oddly romantic about this set-up: the darkness, the music, the occasional beam from a car headlight arcing across the ceiling. And the magic of black on white: words that materialised as if from nowhere, forming sentences, paragraphs, chapters . . . That was something I could never get over. It's so obvious, I know, but it did seem like magic to me: you started with just inked ribbons and typing paper, and you created people, events, places. These were not just images or shadows, but people with histories and futures, feelings and failings, personalities, peccadillos and penchants. And not just places that were familiar, but new towns, cities, landscapes. Even entire new worlds. And events that could change lives, alter destinies. And you were in control. You started with wood pulp and chemical dye and you ended with an alternative universe. No wonder I sat there every night while the rest of the world was asleep; it was the most exciting experience I had ever known.

And if, by chance, as a result of my efforts, I managed to sell the occasional short story, I became delirious with joy. Whilst, like virtue, writing was its own reward, receiving hard cash for my efforts was truly the icing on the cake. I longed for the day when someone would ask me what I did for a living, and I could turn to them and say 'well, it's like this; I sit down and make things up, and someone else pays me for it'. It was already true, to a limited degree, but I knew that I would not feel comfortable about making such a claim until I had sold my first novel.

As things stood, I was just getting by. There were no luxuries in my life; it was very much a hand to mouth existence, and finding enough money to pay the rent and bills was frequently a struggle. But I can't say I was particularly unhappy about it. My meagre savings diminished, but I got by. I suffered the same occasional bouts of despair that afflict every writer, caused, usually, by an inability to string more than three words together successfully. Invariably I would frustrate myself with dreams of hitting the big-time, but all in all, I was satisfied with my lot.

Once a week I would allow myself a day's respite from the heavy business of wordmongering and head to the West End to do the rounds of the second-hand bookshops, up and down the Charing Cross Road.

I soon developed an interest in collecting modern first editions. For the same price as a new paperback I discovered I could usually pick up a fine condition, second-hand hardback copy of the same novel that might, with time, actually increase in value. I was an avid fiction

27

reader, a voracious consumer of other people's lies, and consequently novels were more than just books to me. They were something very special.

I relished these days out, as they seemed to combine a number of pleasurable activities; treasure hunting, shopping, investing, as well as giving me an opportunity to escape the cesspit for a few hours.

Searching for the possible 'earners' soon developed into an obsession, and whilst my funds were limited, I found that, with judicious budgeting, I could usually afford one or two books every week. Before long I was acquainted with virtually every bookshop in WC2, and could find my way from one shop to the next blindfolded. I fell into walking in patterns, and if anyone had bothered to plot my movements, they would soon have discovered the quickest and most time-efficient way of wandering through that part of London.

Some days would find me in ecstasies, having laid my hands on a first edition John Fowles for just a few quid, or an early Ian McEwan for under a tenner. I longed to find a mint condition *Lord of the Flies*, which I knew could fetch three hundred pounds, lying in some grotty basement with a fifty pence price tag attached.

I quickly learned the importance of buying only fine or very good copies; unless it looked like new, or had been read just once, there was virtually no market for it. And as for the subject of dust-wrappers, that was easy. In the world of modern first editions, it was perfectly acceptable to judge a book by its cover: if it didn't have one, it was virtually worthless.

Although I could barely afford this exercise in speculative investment, I justified it by convincing myself that, in buying and selling these books, I could make a small profit and increase my otherwise moribund funds. Alas, it wasn't that simple. The fact was, I couldn't bear to part with my acquisitions. There's something about a hardback novel that makes it difficult to relinquish. I loved the feel of them, the weight, the solidity. In the process of collecting the books I learned about their production, and became even more attached to these marvels of manufacturing; the stitching, the binding, the quality of paper, ink, boards, the jacket . . . Almost regardless of their content, they became valuable objects in their own right, and I was loathe to give up a single one of them. Consequently, rather than increasing my disposable income, all I did was increase my book collection. But I enjoyed it. Perhaps I believed that, one day, I would walk into a bookstore and find my own first novel, nestling in amongst the Goldings and Greenes on the First Editions shelf with a hefty price tag attached, having become a much sought-after collectors' item.

My lack of abundant financial resources did, however, impinge upon my social life and, for the best part of a year, entertainment as such was limited to the occasional night in the pub with Kev and/or various other friends, plus the occasional foray to the cinema. I always accepted dinner invitations (Jenny, knowing my pecuniary status, was especially thoughtful in this regard, and rarely had a dinner party without inviting me) and although I had not, at that time, reached a point where I could reciprocate, nobody ever suggested that I was free-loading. Thankfully, my choice of career and lifestyle meant that I was a welcome dinner guest, frequently the token bohemian or eccentric, depending on the company.

Jenny's friends were a mixed bunch, and over the years she had built up a network of companions, contacts and associates that spanned everything from dogged professionals whose careers meant everything to them, to media types who seemed to talk a different language to everyone else. Consequently, these informal soirées were usually an opportunity to meet the sort of people that one might not otherwise come across in the normal course of existence.

But even on those evenings when I found myself surrounded by arty types, or a couple of would-be non-conformists, it still seemed as if I was truly living in a different world to most of my contemporaries. Most of Jenny's friends found it difficult to relate, at first, to what I was doing with my life, and people who had never met me before often reacted with astonishment. The notion that I had abandoned regular, paid employment to write without any guarantee of success seemed – especially to those who found themselves half-way up career ladders – like the actions of a madman. I saw this sort of response to my way of life as a challenge, and it was a source of considerable pleasure to be able to expound on my own personal philosophies regarding work, creativity and freedom.

I like to think that I was never bombastic, dogmatic or precious when it came to these discussions. If, as happened occasionally, someone took it upon themselves to attack my way of life ('lazy, irresponsible, selfish') then, rather than attack in turn, I would try and find out what it was about my lifestyle that appeared so reprehensible. In this way I hoped to diffuse possible tension whilst at the same time learn something new about human nature.

By the time coffee was being served, attitudes had often changed dramatically. Having told them something about the freedom that comes with opting out, and shared a little about the act of creation and the wonders that accompany it, many of those who had originally lambasted me for being irresponsible seemed a good deal less certain about the value of their own careers. A few, even some who had everything that the modern corporate world could provide, looked set to give it all up and become poets or novelists. Whenever this happened (and it happened more frequently than one might have imagined) I considered it a small victory. If the pen was no longer mightier than the sword, there were at least occasions on which it might topple the expense account. For an evening, anyway.

Inevitably, meeting Cassandra brought about a number of changes in my circumstances, and whilst these were slow to take effect, in time they radically altered the way I led my life. But, as ever, I was slow to see it coming. The reason was simple; I just could not believe whatever it was that Cassandra and I had become embroiled in had any chance of surviving beyond a week or two. Despite finding my sexual thirst satisfied after the long drought, I continued to believe that my life was entirely my own, and that even if this strange and unique woman had made some aspects of that life a little more interesting, there was no reason to suppose that there would be any long lasting repercussions. Whatever it was that bound Cassandra and I together, I did not consider that it was serious and naturally assumed that, like the butt end of a candle, it would burn itself out before long.

In this respect I was quite wrong. Four, five, six weeks passed, with no sign of our relationship deteriorating. How could it? It was already a festering mess, crawling along the bottom of some abandoned gutter; there was really no way it could get any worse. And therein lay the problem. We had little or no respect for each other, cared not a jot about each other's happiness, and neither of us, it seemed, was the least upset about this. We connected at one level, and one level only, and there was never any attempt to shift the relationship on to a higher plane or lift it, for any reason, out of that gutter.

Because it was so extraordinarily one-dimensional, it didn't seem to impinge upon my everyday life at all. For those first six weeks, we lived wholly independently, and twice a week engaged, usually in the dark, on a floor or a bed or a table, and perpetrated various physical acts on each other that the polite world would term making love, but that, in reality, had so little to do with love as to make the description laughable. We did what highly sexed, obsessive animals would do if they had the time, imagination, inclination and energy. We stroked, sucked, poked, prodded, licked, fingered, twisted and pinched. We slapped, smacked, nibbled and bit, and cursed and cried and yelled. And more. Our bodies, collectively, were our playgrounds, our laboratories, in which we could play and experiment and push things to their limits. It was, in whichever way you wish to define the word, fantastic.

I soon became quite accustomed to our strange, other-worldly rituals, to the point where they became habitual, and as much a part of my week as eating, sleeping and working.

With these regular bouts of intimacy, we became familiar not just with each other's bodies, but also with each other's particular predilections in the sexual arena. The 'do's' and 'don'ts' of bedside manner had to be negotiated, although there seemed to be no end to the former and few constraints on the latter. Suffice to say that, despite our continual mutual haranguing and the

32

endless accusations of inability and uselessness, we each learned slowly but surely to pleasure the other in the manner most certain to elicit maximum enjoyment. This was, after all, what it was all about. In this way we did start to learn something about each other's behaviour, albeit in a strictly limited field. Cassandra, you see, had an almost insatiable appetite when it came to matters of the flesh.

I wish I could tell you more about those early days, regale you with tales of fun and frolic, or paint pictures of hazy, romantic evenings spent gazing into one another's eyes over candlelit dinners whilst string quartets played in the background . . . but there was none of that. All I can tell you about is the sex, because that's all there was.

Perhaps you should know about the sex; if you don't know details, then you'll never understand. Not that I'm able – or likely – to relate all of it, or even most of it; there's no room for pornography or titillation here. But there was an occasion, an incident, that was to have grave repercussions. And it's all to do with hopes, wishes and dreams coming true. Dirty dreams.

And a rhinoceros.

4

It was Jenny who first introduced me to the rhinoceros. We had been sitting in Jenny's local, The Salisbury, a couple of weeks after I had first met Cassandra, enjoying a few warming drinks and chatting about this and that. There was a group of four or five of us, and other than the fact that, due to Cassandra, I hadn't seen any of them for two or three weeks (even in my 'celibate hermit' phase I always managed to get to the pub once a week), there was nothing to distinguish the evening from any of a number of similar occasions. We were, however, more than usually garrulous that night; perhaps we all had a lot on our minds. I remember feeling vaguely frustrated; part of me had wanted to tell them about Cassandra. The other part of me, as you know, had already decided against such measures. Instead, I joined in the conversations that were in progress, rarely initiating anything. I was happy just to be with my friends, even if I felt that I was not fully in attendance. Every now and then, my thoughts would drift to Cassandra, and the four or five extraordinary nights we had already spent together.

Jenny, as you know, had recently turned thirty, and during the course of the evening the conversation drifted inevitably to future plans and what we were all going to do with our slowly diminishing lives. Jenny said that her recent birthday had caused a great deal of turmoil and confusion. Whereas previously she had been unconcerned about which direction her life was taking, now that she was thirty she felt less at ease with her happy-go-lucky attitude. She thought she should be applying herself to a definite goal. Time was moving on and she never wanted to be in a position of looking back on her life and cursing because she had not achieved anything significant. This, in turn, led on to a general discussion about what comprised a significant achievement. Kev reckoned that bedding ten beautiful women in a single year was about the zenith of his personal achievements to date and could think of nothing higher to aim for. Sally, Kev's date, gave him a stiff dig in the ribs and stormed off. Mike, Jenny's recently acquired boyfriend, confessed that he had virtually no ambition, and as long as he could continue working and had enough money to pay the bills and go on one decent holiday a year, he'd be satisfied.

I, on the other hand, admitted to being wildly ambitious. I stated it bluntly: I wanted to write a massive international literary bestseller that was not only critically acclaimed, not only made me a household name but also brought in enough revenue that I need never worry about money again.

And that's when Jenny said it.

'Don't wish for a rhinoceros unless you've got a big backyard.'

There was a moment's pause, an almost breathless silence, then everyone laughed.

'What's that supposed to mean?' chipped in Kev.

Jenny's brow furrowed, 'Just that. If you desire great things, just make sure you're prepared for them.'

35

'You make it sound like a curse,' I said.

'I suspect it is,' replied Jenny. 'These things are never simple, are they? How many times do you read about how miserable the wealthy and famous are, how they lose their humanity, become drug addicts, recluses, estranged . . .'

'That's very negative,' I said. 'You just never hear about the happy, successful ones. It's like good news: no one's interested.' Jenny's attitude peeved me; success seemed an elusive enough goal as it was without people dismissing it out of hand.

'Perhaps,' said Jenny. 'Or maybe the happy, successful ones are those with the big backyard.' She looked at me then, intently, concerned. 'Don't underestimate the power of wishing, Bill. Ambition can be a dangerous thing. I don't believe in God or fairies or genies, but one thing I do know is that, if you want something enough, it has a nasty habit of coming true.'

Kev laughed. 'It's never been that easy for me.'

'You got your ten beautiful women, didn't you?'

'Yeah, but not because . . .'

'Wait a minute,' I interrupted. 'You really believe wishes come true?'

Jenny nodded. 'If you really want something enough, if you direct all your will towards it . . . yeah, I think so. But never the way you envisage it . . . unless you're careful.'

'What do you mean, *careful*.'

'Being prepared, thinking it through, thinking about all the possible repercussions. Wishing aimlessly, carelessly . . . that's just asking for trouble. That's like wanting your dreams to come true.'

Mike frowned. 'Don't you want your dreams to come true?'

Jenny laughed, but it was a cynical laugh, without any joy or pleasure. 'Are you kidding? Most of the dreams I have – or at least, those that I remember – scare me witless.'

'You should eat less cheese . . .'

'I'm serious,' said Jenny. 'I'm very careful about what I wish for.'

'You're just timid,' I said. 'Like my mother. She once confessed to me that, before she went to sleep, she would wish for a win on the premium bonds. Every night, she'd make a wish that she'd win five thousand pounds. When she told me about this I said to her, "If you're going to go to the trouble of wishing for a win, then why not wish for a hundred thousand pounds. At least make it worthwhile." I remember her shaking her head very seriously; "Oh no", she said; "that would be greedy." '

Mike and Kev laughed, but Jenny just smiled. 'She's very wise, your mum.'

'What! Why?' She was getting to me now. There were times when Jenny elevated the practice of being a wet blanket into an art-form.

'Because . . . ,' she began, then paused dramatically. 'If you wish for a rhinoceros . . .'

'Yeah yeah . . . big backyard.' Jenny smiled, but I was still scowling. 'I think you're crazy. This is a ridiculous conversation anyway; wishing for something doesn't make it happen.'

'Kid's got a point there,' said Kev, ever the pragmatist. He raised his empty glass and gave it a little shake in the perfectly reasonable assumption that whoever's turn it was to buy the round would do his or her duty. Perhaps he should have wished a little harder, because whilst Jenny had the floor, no one was moving.

37

'You think so? Next time you have some spare time Bill, think back to all the major events in your life, and see if they weren't preceded, in some way or another, by you wishing for them to happen. I think you'll be surprised.'

'I'll be bloody amazed,' I said, with rather more venom than necessary. I can't imagine why I was so upset about it. I headed to the bar to get the next round and, when I returned, the conversation had shifted to something altogether less controversial.

Whilst I professed not to take any of what Jenny had said very seriously, I had to admit that the image of the rhino stayed with me for several days. So much so, that on one particularly creativity-free evening, I sat down and made a list of all the crucial events that had happened to me since my sixteenth birthday. I don't know why I chose that as a starting point; there was no great logic to it, although I had this sense that it wasn't until I turned sixteen that I began to believe that an individual might have some control over his or her own destiny. Whatever, having made the list, I separated all those events into two groups: those that had been, by and large, good, valuable or enjoyable, and those that had been unpleasant, damaging or just plain bad. And then I examined each individually. Which of these events had I actively planned? Had any of them been purely seren-dipitous? How many had started off as simple wishes, desires, day-dreams?

I tried to be scrupulously honest in my assessment and recall and, having amassed all the details, I then attempted to analyse the data and see if there was any-thing to Jenny's claim. What I discovered was both unlikely and astonishing.

A week later, by chance, I saw an interview on

television with Mother Theresa. A film crew had been sent to Calcutta to document her work amongst the poor, the homeless, the sick and the dying. As is the way with such documentaries, many of the scenes were disturbing and harrowing. I'm sure, like many others, the only reason I continued to watch, to put up with these terrible scenes of degradation and despair, was to catch sight of this tiny, wizened, miraculous woman. Her courage and fortitude in the face of such overwhelming horror was remarkable, and when questioned as to where she received her seemingly limitless energy, she conceded that it came from God, and that prayer sustained her. When she was asked if she felt that God answered her prayers, she gave a sigh and nodded, rather sadly. The interviewer was clearly puzzled; surely this was what everyone wished for, to have their prayers answered. Mother Theresa smiled sadly. When someone's prayers are answered, she said softly, that is when their problems really begin . . .

Sometimes, a person just doesn't take a hint. And more often than not, that person is me. The fact was, there was a rhinoceros bearing down on me at that very moment, and I didn't even have a window-box, let alone a big backyard.

Sigmund Freud built his reputation on theories concerning when and where our adult sexual predilections originate. Over the years, people have seen fit to disagree with him, not least his own disciples such as Jung and Reich. Unfortunately, I had never felt either sufficiently well versed or interested in psychology to figure out who was closest, in my own humble estimation, to the truth of the matter. One thing I did know, however, was that there were certain things of a sexual nature – or rather, one particular act – that I had wanted to experience ever since losing my virginity, but had never admitted to anyone. Not to my partners, not to my mates, not to anyone. I still recall the first time I thought of it, and how, despite the fact that no one else could possibly have known what was going on in the private realms of my thoughts, I blushed with shame and embarrassment. Not just bashfulness or sheepishness; I was deeply ashamed. Ashamed, even, that I was capable of such disgusting and depraved thoughts. Such disgusting, depraved and exciting thoughts. I could neither ignore them nor admit them, and neither, it seemed, could I do anything about them. I certainly had not wanted to investigate where such desires originated, as I suspected they had hatched in some rather dark, murky part of my psyche which was best left undisturbed. Don't get the wrong idea; I'm not talking about anything abominable – no animals or children or anything like that ... God knows, I wasn't totally depraved. It's just ... there were just ... I just ...

We all have our fantasies, right?

We just don't expect them to come true.

It was a Friday night. I arrived at Cassandra's place just after dark, having put in a fairly respectable day's work at the typewriter. I was in good spirits, looking forward to the evening ahead; it was still early days in our relationship, and the excitement of this novel liaison was at its height.

I found Cassandra in a less than happy mood; she was also clearly drunk. She had not been home for very long; just enough time to strip off her clothes, put on a silk robe and polish off half a bottle of gin. At least. She opened up the conversation with her usual plethora of expletives, accusing me of lateness yet again. Apparently I had proved once more that I was a totally unreliable individual (these were not her exact words) and that if I couldn't be bothered to keep a date I might just as well 'fuck off' (verbatim, this time).

Did she want me to leave? I asked, all smiles. We didn't know much about each other then, but I knew that a cheery smile was guaranteed to rile her.

'Oh for fuck's sake!' she screamed. 'Don't you under-stand? I've had a shit of a day . . .'

Although I was not in the least interested, Cassandra went on to relate, briefly, the contents of her shitty day. How she had had to deal with three thoroughly obnoxious guests who had spent two hours complaining about the lack of service at the hotel's main restaurant. That quite frankly, despite her position, she couldn't really have given a flying fuck, and almost told them the same. It was only the knowledge that she would be able to abuse me later that kept her from losing her temper. She hadn't eaten all day and consequently had been drinking on an empty stomach. So much for the glam-orous world of Public Relations. As far as I was concerned, she could keep it.

I listened to all this half-heartedly as Cassandra shoved me into the darkened living room, aware only that her robe was flapping back and forth, affording me tantalising glimpses of her milk-white thighs.

She told me to help myself to a drink, ordered me to pour her one, then tripped over the carpet. This was always a risk, drunk or not. She would never have the lights on when I was around, and we did everything in semi-darkness. Anyway, needless to say, I burst out laughing. Cassandra scowled, and hurled her empty

41

glass, which missed me by a whisker and crashed into the wall just a few inches behind my head.

'You stupid cow!' I yelled. 'You could have had my eye out!'

But clearly Cassandra was taking no more notice of what I said than I had of her. In a moment she had crossed the room and was all over me.

Cassandra had to be some sort of medal-winner when it came to kissing. With hands clasped tightly on either side of my face, she employed a teasing, breathy technique which, whilst difficult to describe and impossible to emulate, nevertheless would have me aroused and raring to go within seconds. Tonight, the alcohol had evidently loosened her considerably, and in addition to her displays of manual and oscular dexterity, she began to talk dirty. This was a new experience for me, and hearing that Hampstead accent wrap itself around words like 'prick' and 'cunt' was oddly surreal, like hearing a nun swear.

We soon found ourselves on the living room floor, rolling around in a passionate clinch. I had learned on our first encounter that Cassandra was a good deal stronger than she appeared, and that she could summon up extra reserves of energy at will so that, if one were wrestling with her, she could quite easily get the upper hand. It was one of the elements of our entanglement that made sex so exciting. She was also very commanding; nothing weak-willed or namby pamby about Cassandra's wants and desires. On this occasion she was soon unzipping my flies and prising me, not in the least delicately, out of my boxers. Keeping one very careful eye on her (you never knew what she might do and, as I mentioned, she had remarkably sharp teeth) I tried to manoeuvre myself into a comfortable position, but as

Cassandra had shouldered me up against the wall, this was no easy task. I had one hand up her robe, whilst the other was busy assisting her to get my trousers off.

'No,' she snapped. 'Leave that to me.'

As ever, I did as I was told. Cassandra had a passion for undressing me. I had not previously met a woman who was so keen to see me naked, and it was a revelation to discover someone who was as fascinated and preoccupied with my genitalia as I was.

Once my trousers and boxer shorts had been removed and propelled to the other side of the room, she had me stand upright whilst she knelt in front of me. She maintained this position for some time, her hands grasping my buttocks, staring at my erection and breathing heavily. I tried, gently, to coerce her into a more active participation, but she just slapped my hand away. Continuing to clutch my backside with her left hand, her right hand disappeared down between her legs. I tried to push her robe off her shoulders, but this was evidently out of bounds too. She cursed me a couple of times, then started to outline in explicit detail what she wanted me to do to her, some of which sounded a little far-fetched, even by my reckoning. She started to stroke me then, and continued with her frank exposition of what we were, any moment now, about to do to each other. All the while she fixed her attention entirely on my groin, while her hands motioned back and forth with increasing fervour. Every muscle in my body was tensed and sweat started to run in desperate little rivulets down my body.

After a minute of this I was almost insane with desire. Much to my surprise I discovered that there was something intensely arousing about being used as a sex aid; for a moment I half expected her to get out a camera and make me pose while she took provocative Polaroids of me. But my body was aching now with the need for release, and there was no way I could keep my hands off her for much longer.

And then, just as things were getting out of control, she said it; the key to my dark, distasteful fantasy. I couldn't quite believe it; just dirty talk, just games, right? But no, it was not a game, not a trick. Without another word, she turned and, still kneeling, gathered her robe up around her waist, bowed down until her forehead was touching the floor. With her perfectly proportioned rump glistening in the half-light, she commanded me to do that which I had hungered for most of my adult life. My dirty dream had just come true. With the blood thumping in my temples, driven by a furious, bestial lust and with not a moment's concern for either the moral or statutory laws that I was surely about to violate, I fell to my knees and grabbed her roughly around the waist. With the salty sweat stinging my eyes, I thrust deeply into that long forbidden territory, and I did not stop, not until my body, racked with the exertions, fell away, spent and exhausted.

She yelped at one point, perhaps in pain, perhaps in pleasure. I never did ask her.

From that moment on, I was hers. Cassandra, Cassandra, Cassandra. Cassandra had made my dirty dreams come true, and now there was nothing that I would not do for her.

We stayed in the house all weekend. By the time Monday morning arrived I was so sore and so exhausted that I thought I'd never be able to engage in any form of sexual activity ever again.

The following weekend soon put paid to such thoughts.

* * *

I sometimes wonder whether Cassandra knew. Had she somehow managed to look into those dark, grubby realms of my soul and seen my deepest secret? And had she then deliberately enticed me, like a spider to a fly, knowing that I could not resist and that, once caught, I would be forever trapped; a victim of my unholiest desires, a slave to the most savage parts of my nature. Because one thing is certain. If you need to plot the graph of my decline, then this is where the line first begins to dip. Even though I could not possibly know it at the time, from here on, it was downhill all the way. It seems absurd that anyone would debase themselves in such a way, but then, you don't know Cassandra; you don't know what she was capable of. There was so much more to her than met the eye. Of course I'll never know for sure, not now.

But I still wonder.

When someone's prayers are answered, that is when their problems really begin.

And I had my very own rhinoceros lurking around to prove it.

5

There are many things on my mind, things which must
be said if you are ever to understand my predicament. I
do not wish to censor my thoughts; I don't want to hold
anything back. I have nothing left to hide. I want to
make broad, seemingly unsupportable generalisations. I
want to knock you down with sweeping statements and
bowl you over with outrageous hyperbole. This is the
only language that will be of any use; it is the only
language that will make sense.

To begin. Men do not understand women. Hardly an
original observation, but true none the less. It isn't
because they don't try (although most don't) or because
they don't want to understand (ditto), but simply
because men cannot understand women. They have neither the acuteness of sensitivity nor the depth of em-
pathy required for such an action. Men aren't built
that way, which is why even those that try, fail. It's all to
do with this thing called *adaequatio*. I know about
adaequatio thanks, in a roundabout sort of way, to Cassandra. It is all to do with one of her little 'jokes'.

There were times when, rather than being downright
abusive, Cassandra simply wanted to remind me of how
she really felt about me. Fair enough; it was well within
the ground rules. Unfortunately, the method she chose

for these little exercises in realism was to interject at sensitive moments these really petty, niggling little insults, that were hardly insults at all, but were spoken with just enough venom to hurt. I believe that, rather than forming part of her mighty attack armoury, these particular slights were, rather, minor elements in her extensive battery of defences. I say this because the time she liked to use them most of all was after sex, when she was theoretically at her most vulnerable. Let's face it, it could be a problem. Sex was the only time when we were both susceptible to the possibility of closeness or affection and whilst I don't recall, even in the beginning, showing any especial care or tenderness towards Cassandra in the afterglow, clearly she was not taking any chances. As a result, following any act of sexual congress, even if she had been screaming with pleasure just moments earlier, as soon as she was able to utter a word clearly, the first thing she would do is look me in the eyes, then look down at my detumescing penis and give a little smirk. And with just enough caustic undertone to kill the possibility of laughter, she'd say: 'Oh well, you know what they say; small is beautiful.'

It soon became a habit. It wasn't funny the first time, and it never became any better. 'Oh well, small is beautiful,' she'd say, and I'd clench my teeth in irritation. If I responded out loud, in any way, she accused me of being defensive or over-sensitive or, on one occasion, of being 'a poncey, pathetic, little-dicked wimp'. (Why use just one adjective when three will do the job, right?) Whatever, this knowing little quip soon began to get on my nerves.

There were, of course, variations on a theme: Cassandra was nothing if not creative. For one whole week I was awarded a new appellation that seemingly put me up there in the pantheon of Great Mississippi Blues Singers: Muddy Waters, Blind Lemon Jefferson and ('Ladies and Gentlemen, put your hands together for . . .') *Shrivelling Willy*.

It was tedious but, compared to some of Cassandra's other epithets for me, relatively harmless. Besides, she soon tired of it and before long we were back to 'Oh well . . . small is beautiful.'

After about a fortnight of this and, having become stupefyingly accustomed to hearing it, I suddenly realised that I really didn't know anything about the expression; I didn't know where it originated and, more to the point, I didn't know what it meant. That it was 'in circulation' was apparent; I had come across it before Cassandra's wholesale adoption of it for her own spiteful purposes. But as to its true meaning, I didn't have a clue. And, I suspected, neither did Cassandra. So I endeavoured to find out.

It was Jenny who identified the source for me.

'It's Schumacher's,' she said in a manner which clearly indicated that this was all that needed to be said. Alas, whilst I considered myself educated, well-read and reasonably intelligent, this did not strike up any immediate associations save for the unfortunate literal translation from the German: 'cobblers'.

'Schumachers?' I replied after a moment's hesitation, a frown of concentration signalling that yes, it sounded familiar, but I couldn't quite place it. The vision of elderly shoemakers, clad in *lederhosen*, bent over their lasts still danced uncomfortably in the forefront of my mind.

'Yes, you know,' said Jenny, making huge assumptions about my general knowledge and sparing me the embarrassment of displaying my ignorance further.

'E. F. Schumacher, the economist. The original Green Guru. Appropriate technology and all that.'

'Oh right,' I said, nodding as if the penny had finally dropped.

'*Small is Beautiful* was the book that really made his name; I'm surprised you haven't read it.'

'Must have passed me by,' I shrugged.

Jenny nodded as if, despite the fact that everyone in the civilised world had read Mr Schumacher, that I had somehow missed out was perfectly understandable. 'Actually, I think I've got a copy upstairs, if you're interested. Hang on.'

Jenny disappeared upstairs for a couple of minutes and returned clutching a handful of paperbacks. 'There you go; they're all pretty interesting. Let me have them back when you've finished.'

I did, but not before I had devoured their contents. There were four books in all and, as Jenny had implied, Schumacher was an interesting writer. So much so that, having read and, I hoped, understood the basic premise of *Small is Beautiful* (which, I was relieved to discover, had nothing to do with genitalia and a great deal to do with economics), I went on to read the others. By far the most intriguing was Schumacher's personal and highly singular book of philosophical musings *A Guide For the Perplexed* which was in turn fascinating, thought provoking and completely loopy.

However, in amongst the many theories and postulates that he drew on to delineate his own, particular world-view, was the simple and, to me, highly pertinent concept of *adaequatio*. Schumacher had appropriated it, in part, from the Greek philosopher Plotinus who, sometime before 270 AD when he abruptly kicked the bucket, was wont to say things such as 'Knowing demands the organ fitted to the object'. Now I appreciate that at first glance this may well sound like the punchline to a not very good smutty joke, but it's all very basic really; you cannot know something unless you have the appropriate instrument to detect it. In a rather more poetic phrase, Plotinus said: 'Never did eye see the sun unless it had first become sunlike, and never can the soul have vision of the First Beauty unless itself be beautiful.' This sort of slightly arch saying may well leave you cold, but believe me, when I first read it it resonated in a way that made me feel as if, despite the 1700 years that separated us, Plotinus had peeked into my heart and extracted a truth that I had long known but had never verbalised to my, or indeed anyone else's satisfaction.

Have you ever seen those photographs of the earth taken on heat sensitive film, highlighting in bright colours the hot spots on the earth's surface? Or, using the same process, the picture of a little boy sitting on a stone step, identifying that his bottom, coloured icy blue in the infra-red photograph, is some several degrees colder than the rest of his body? They're great photos because they reveal aspects of our world that we are unable to know through our usual five senses. Our eyes do not respond to infra-red, so we don't see it. It is there, it is real, but we remain blind to it because we do not have, as Schumacher would put it, the appropriate instrument with which to recognise it.

I tell you, after reading that chapter on *adaequatio* the world suddenly became a much clearer place. It wasn't a religious conversion – I did not, for instance, feel that I could now conquer the world or walk through it unscathed – but it was a minor revelation. And although

I did not, at the time, apply it wholeheartedly to that area of human existence to which it is most appropriate, it was not long before I started to see its relevance. One thing is certain; I sure do now. Men are not *adequate* to the task of understanding women. They're just not fitted with the appropriate equipment. You might just as well ask a dung beetle to understand an elephant, or a honeysuckle to behold a hummingbird. It's not on, is it? And men do not appreciate women, since appreciation is a natural extension of understanding; without comprehension, there can be no appreciation. And without appreciation, things become devalued, and before you know it . . . you see how complicated this all gets?

A friend of mine has this theory. When God created the world, having got the earth, the heavens, the seas the birds, the bees and the apples in order, He created man in His own image . . . and then got bored witless. So he created woman. Not for man's sake, not so that poor, pathetic, defenceless man could have a companion, but so that God could have something to occupy his time, of which there was a good deal. Eternity, to be precise. God has consequently spent since time immemorial watching man attempting to understand woman. And failing. This is otherwise known as 'the history of the world'.

It reminds me of another story I once heard. A famous sculptor, having created a work of infinite beauty, put it on display in a local park. He sat beside the sculpture and watched the adoring public gaze in awe and astonishment at his creation. One particularly smitten character, having studied the sculpture for some considerable time, eventually approached the sculptor and in reverent tones said: 'This is the most wondrous object I have ever set eyes upon; it is beautiful, compelling, extraordinary.

But . . . what is it?' The sculptor looked again at his own creation and shrugged. 'No idea. You tell me.'

It must be inferred, thus, that God is neither omniscient nor omnipotent; just rather immature. Just like men.

Men do not understand women. And I did not understand Cassandra, despite my efforts. And God knows (ha-ha) I tried.

It's getting dark now; it gets dark early here, and I have no idea what, if anything, goes on at night. What's more, I haven't eaten all day. It's easy to forget about mundane matters like eating and drinking when there are so many more important things to take up one's time. I'll have to go out and investigate. I hope I can find somewhere cheap; my funds are limited and who knows where I'll get more money when this lot runs out. But . . . that's a while away. So, tonight I shall eat. And then?

And then I must face what may well turn out to be the longest night in my entire life. I have an empty bed in a strange room in a foreign land, and I am completely and utterly alone, with nothing to keep me company but my own thoughts . . .

I'd better get drunk.

6

When six weeks had passed Cassandra invited me to move in with her. Well, it wasn't so much an invitation as an order. 'You'll have to move in. I can't stand the thought of you living in that pigsty,' she said. A pigsty, incidentally, that she had never once laid eyes on. It must be said that she caught me with my guard down. I, mistakenly, assumed this was a show of genuine concern – the first I had seen from Cassandra – and I was quite taken aback.

It didn't occur to me then that she was serious. It was only when she told me to get off my arse and get a move on that the penny dropped.

'You want me to move in with you.'

'What makes you think that?' she sneered; sarcasm never strayed far from Cassandra; it hung in the air around her like a bad smell. 'Ah, wait a moment. Could it be anything to do with my half dozen invitations? Don't let anyone tell you that you're not on the ball, William.'

'It's Bill. And I didn't think you were serious.'

'Less thought dear boy, more action. Now do get yourself in gear or you'll miss the expiry date.'

'I'll think about it.'

'What is there to think about? I've made you a

perfectly good offer with no strings attached. Now, yes or no?'

'Stop pestering me, will you? I said I'd give it some thought, what more do you want?'

She took a deep breath. I think I must have sensed what was coming. 'What is wrong with you?' she said, a rather harder edge to her voice now. 'You do understand what's being offered here, hmm? Or is it a bit complicated? You know, when we first met, I could have sworn there was a glimmer of sympathetic intelligence lurking behind those deep blue eyes. Just goes to show, eh? You know William, tall dark and handsome isn't everything . . .'

'You patronising cow. Why don't you just lay off for a while. I said I'd think about it.'

'You are sorely trying my patience.'

'But Cassandra . . .'

'What? What is it?' she snapped. There was a sudden intolerance in her voice, verging on anger. This was the thing about Cassandra; for most of the time I knew her, she was on a very short fuse. 'Oh for Godsake, stop looking like a forlorn puppy that's lost its mother. Do you intend moving in or not? I'll be quite clear about this William. It's becoming very inconvenient having you stuck out there in the back of beyond. I can't spend my life giving you lifts back and forth; I have a busy enough schedule most days as it is. If you honestly value that wretched squat more than me . . . Well, it beggars belief. I mean it's hardly as if you're giving anything up, are you? I'd have thought you'd be delighted. I can name a dozen young men who would jump at the chance . . .'

'Okay okay okay,' I said, holding up my hands to bring this harangue to a conclusion. There was never any discussion with Cassandra; either you did things her way or not at all. I decided the easiest thing was to agree. After all, the bedsit really was a cesspit, and Cassandra's place was a good deal more comfortable. It might even be fun. Didn't all the famous London writers live in Hampstead? Who knows who I might bump into whilst out jogging on the Heath on a Sunday morning? At the very least it would be a change of scenery and, in one fell swoop, it would abolish the rather structured timetable of our sex-life. At the time, our twice weekly bouts of thrashing around were scheduled like doctor's appointments; it did rather take the spontaneity out of things. And if it didn't work I could always move out again.

So, that afternoon, I packed up my clothes, my typewriter, my electric kettle and my cassettes, put my books into storage, said goodbye to my landlady (regretting that I never got around to doing a Raskolnikov on her) and moved into Cassandra's Hampstead home. That weekend Cassandra threw out all my clothes. And then she took me shopping.

Now, this was certainly a new experience for me. Sure, I'd had clothes bought for me, but not since I was a kid, when my mother would drag me kicking and screaming to get the new school uniform. I hated those shops with their fusty décor and snooty sales assistants who made no attempt to conceal the fact that they hated little boys. After being pulled and pushed, shoved and jostled, coaxed, cajoled and squeezed into a selection of too-tight trousers or baggy blazers, it always came down to the same thing. Nothing fitted. And when things didn't fit it was my fault. 'Well madam,' was the usual rejoinder; 'he's an unusual size for an eleven-year-old, isn't he?'

Was I? Admittedly, I was tall for my age, but so what?

Kids grew at different rates, didn't they? And if I didn't fit into an eleven-year-old's uniform, what was the problem with putting me in a thirteen-year-old's? My mother, bless her, would sigh. 'You're growing so fast; you'll end up costing us a fortune.'

And this was how it continued throughout my early teens. No matter what item of clothing I tried on, it was never right. Jackets fitted across the chest but shrank away from my extended, skinny wrists; trousers fitted snugly around the waist but flapped around somewhere between ankle and shin. And shoes, of course, were always uncomfortable.

So it was that from an early age, shopping for clothes was an activity infused with trauma; if clothes didn't fit, it was my fault. If they were too expensive, that was my fault too. I recoiled every time I heard my mother say: 'That old jacket/coat/whatever doesn't fit you any more; we'll have to get you a new one.' These words were like an invitation to hell.

In later years girlfriends would buy me gifts of sweaters and shirts. That was fine with me. As long as I didn't have to go traipsing around the stores, suffering the indignity of being told that something 'doesn't quite hang right' I didn't care. People could buy me whatever they wanted and I would wear said gifts with pleasure and gratitude. You see, I just *hated* shopping for clothes.

So when Cassandra decided to take me on just such an expedition, she didn't realise what she was letting herself in for. I tried to warn her, but she chided me for being stupid.

'For goodness sake, I can't have you walking around like something that's just been run over by a truck. Now stop being such a pain.'

'Why don't you listen to me! I've just told you, I don't want to do this.'

'What you do or do not want is, I'm afraid to say, of no especial consequence in this matter.'

'Or any other matter, it seems . . .'

'Don't be petulant William, it doesn't suit you.'

'Fuck off Cassandra. I will not be bullied.'

'Charmed, I'm sure. Really William, you quite surpass yourself with these rare, literary expletives. But then, I forget . . . you're a *writer*, aren't you?'

'You sarcastic bitch.'

'They just keep coming, don't they. Well, much as I'd love to stand here all day listening to you exercising your creative muscle by reeling off these sparkling locutions, I regret that I have more important things to do. And so do you. Now, let's get a move on, shall we?'

'But Cassandra . . . look, I'll spell it out for you. I just don't like going shopping . . .'

'I'm not discussing it any further with you, William. If you wish to be seen out in public with me then you must look respectable, and as you have no clothes of your own that could, by any manner or means, be considered respectable, I have offered, as an act of good will, to kit you out with some half-way decent apparel. We're going shopping, and that's all there is to it. My God, you're so ungrateful; anyone else would have been delighted. After all, it's not as if it's costing you anything . . .'

That was the thing about Cassandra, as I was to discover later; although she never complained about the fact that she was spending money on me, she always alluded to it, just to let me know that I was being 'looked after'.

So, with no arguments to counter her, I allowed myself for the first time since those early teenage years to be dragged from store to store like a miserable, spoilt child, and once again I was made to feel like a freak. But not, this time, by the staff. 'Oh do grow up!' Cassandra yelled at me in one particular store when I refused to try on a yellow and black sweater on the grounds that it made me look like an over-ripe banana.

Still, Cassandra – as you have probably ascertained by now – had a remarkably resilient character. And money was no object. We visited only the best department stores and most fashionable men's shops. I had never previously had a reason to wander down Regent Street other than to get as quickly as possible from Oxford Circus to Piccadilly. By the time Cassandra had finished with me I knew it like the back of my hand.

During that afternoon, among other things, I tried on no less than ten pairs of designer jeans, three of which were considered suitable. I wouldn't have minded so much if Cassandra hadn't insisted on patting my bottom every time she found a pair that suited me. 'Mmmm,' she would purr, slapping my rump with delight, 'those fit just perfectly'. This little routine amused the sales assistants no end, whilst reducing me to a blushing, stammering wreck. The women watching this would giggle outright, whilst the men looked on with a mixture of embarrassment and what could only be (of all things) envy. Despite the humiliation I felt, I could just about understand their reactions. Cassandra looked like every man's dream; who wouldn't want to be petted and patted in public by such a gorgeous and evidently wealthy woman? I suppose I should have played up to it, but my phobia of shopping for clothes just made the whole experience one long trial.

In addition to the jeans, Cassandra bought me a number of shirts, sweaters, jackets, ties, a pair of dress trousers, skimpy underwear (Cassandra was the first woman I had met who could genuinely be described as a voyeur) and three pairs of shoes. She also insisted on buying me a suit. I had never owned a suit; I had never worn one.

'What on earth for?'

'Stop whining; you'll look lovely in it.'

'But why do I need a suit?'

'Because it's necessary; do stop being so cantankerous. What do you know about these things anyway? Really, you have all the dress-sense of a tramp. Now come along.'

She took me to get my hair cut, my beard trimmed, my fingernails manicured. I was to be a new man. She joked that she was going to have my dick dyed bright orange too. And by that stage, I wasn't sure she didn't mean it.

So what brought on this extraordinary show of generosity? What made Cassandra want to spend a small fortune, dressing me up like a shop-window dummy? Did she think, perhaps, that I was sick of living like a pauper and that a few new sets of clothes might make me feel better? Did she believe that I was embarrassed by my appearance, by my lack of smart attire? No, of course not. She couldn't care less how I felt. I was being tarted up because *she* was embarrassed, simple as that. Our liaison was no longer to be kept secret. I was moving in with her, about to become an accepted part of Cassandra's life and, as I stood, I did not 'fit'. I was not fit to be seen in public with her. I did not match expectations; I did not look right. Friends, acquaintances, family; they all knew that she had met someone, and she could no longer keep my identity, or indeed my corporeality, a secret. I had to be introduced. Paraded. Presented. And, therefore, I had to be presentable.

Of course, she needn't have gone to so much trouble. She could have given me the elbow, and that would have solved a number of problems. But she didn't. Of course, I had no inkling then of what Cassandra had in store. If I had known, things might have been very different.

But I doubt it.

So, newly adorned, I made my appearance on the social scene. I 'came out' with all the pomp and cere-mony afforded a débutante. My debut was to take place the following night at a cocktail party held by one of Cassandra's business associates at his sumptuous apart-ment in Knightsbridge. This was considered a safe bet; there would be dozens of people milling around, all trying to make an impression and consequently, so Cas-sandra informed me, I would be more or less invisible. I was instructed to wear the suit, not drink too much, and say as little as possible. I assumed this was all a big joke and, as I always liked to please, I laughed.

'What's funny?'

'Huh?'

'I asked you what you found so amusing?'

'Well . . . all of it. I mean, you can't seriously expect me to go to a party in a suit. I mean, it's a party! You can't go to a party in a suit. And as for expecting me to keep quiet and lay off the drink, well . . . your friends will think I'm some sort of boring old fart.'

'They're not my friends, they're acquaintances, and I'd rather they thought you elegant, boring and well-mannered than scruffy, prattling and pissed. Is that clear?'

'Oh fuck off Cassandra; you're not my mother.'

'You ingrate. I ask you to do just one favour for me,

and what do I get? My God, anyone would think I was insisting you give up your freedom for eternity rather than just requesting one evening of your precious time.'

'It's the principle . . .'

'Fuck the principle, William. All I'm asking is that you behave reasonably. Is that so much to ask?'

'It isn't William, it's Bill. And it isn't what you're asking, it's the manner in which you ask it. I'm not your pet to be ordered about.'

Cassandra glared at me. 'Oh for Godsake, if you're going to get into a state every time I ask you a little favour because of your hypersensitivity . . . Look, I'm really not prepared to discuss this any further. You know what's required of you, let's leave it at that.'

Which we did. Until the evening in question, that is, when some little devil inside me decided to rebel against what I saw as an infringement of personal liberties. I told Cassandra that, thanks all the same, I did not want to attend her dumb cocktail party.

'What are you talking about?'

'I don't feel like going.'

'I beg your pardon?'

'The party. I'd rather not go.'

Cassandra narrowed her eyes, weighing me up for a few moments. 'This is some sort of joke, I take it. Well I'm sorry, but I'm not in the mood.'

'No, I'm not joking; I don't want to go to some dull party where I don't know a soul, especially if I have to stand around all night in a strait-jacket sipping Coke. I don't want to go.'

'Don't be ridiculous.'

'But Cassandra . . .'

'Stop simpering. I really do hate it when you do that. Now, I'm in a hurry, so get a move on.'

'Look, this really isn't my sort of thing . . .'

'Oh sweet Jesus!' she yelled, so loudly and aggressively that it took me completely by surprise. 'Don't you understand? I'm not overly keen either. It's a duty; I have to go. You are my escort. It's very simple. There is nothing to discuss. Now stop moaning about it and get ready.'

And that was the end of the discussion. Suddenly I had been swept into a world where 'duties', whatever they might be, took immediate precedence over personal preferences. I was now ensconced in a household where this was the norm, and presumably (although Cassandra did not state it in so many words) if I wished to remain a part of the household, then I had to accommodate such criteria.

I was thus confronted by a fairly straightforward choice. Decline Cassandra's invitation to the ball and risk the full extent of her wrath, followed, no doubt, by being booted back onto the street, or indulge her this one time, making it clear that under no circumstances was she to make assumptions about my attendance to such events in the future without full consultation. As Cassandra had clearly been expecting me to attend, and as it was almost certainly too late for her to find a replacement, I chose the latter action, and just hoped to hell that the evening would not be too much of a bore.

Like the good little boy that I was, I went to the wardrobe, took out the suit, and put it on. It fitted me like a glove but felt about as comfortable as a suit of armour.

So, bedecked in all my finery, and with one of the most stunning women in London on my arm, I entered the rarefied atmosphere of the Knightsbridge Cocktail Party, and I was introduced thus:

'This is Doctor William Schmidt; he's a writer.'
Doctor!

Well, I had to hand it to her. Cassandra could twist the truth and make whatever she desired from it. As a devotee of all things fictional, I could not help but admire her. She went up in my estimation.

'This is Doctor William Schmidt,' she said, time and again that evening, with such confidence and clarity that even I believed her. You see, she even changed my name. As I had told her several times, my name is Bill; I was christened 'Bill'.

And it isn't Schmidt, either.

7

At night this place is like any other city in the world; the night-time hides its true character, disguises the dreary vistas, camouflages the rot and detritus and bathes everything in a fancy-dress costume of neon lights. Shop and food-stall owners ply their deceitful trade whilst holiday-makers promenade up and down, drunk on the atmosphere, the strangeness, the foreignness. They look at everything but see nothing; the real sights – poverty, vice, corruption – pass them by. The cacophony of city noises makes conversation impossible, but they don't care, their ears tuned in to music of another kind, music that I cannot hear. The only thing we have in common are the smells; there's no denying them; the sweet and the sickly, the pungent and the odoriferous, the foul and decaying. And behind them all, lingering in the darkness like a half-remembered dream, the smell of pine needles, dry and crisp, persisting in the warm evening air.

I watch them strolling, hand in hand, arm in arm, along the main drag, carefree, contented . . . untroubled. I watch them gather at cafés and restaurants where they wave to other, similar beings, and raise their glasses across the room. I see them order, pick and choose, and laugh and smile. And later; eating too much food with too much oil off too many plates, for which they are being charged too much money. And they sit there nodding and lip-smacking, keeping up the charade that the food is good, the atmosphere divine and that they are having a wonderful time.

But I know the truth. I've seen it all before. They can hardly wait until the meal is over so they can order coffee to take away the foul taste that's in their mouths, and then go to bed dreaming of fish and chips and a decent cup of tea.

I'm not sleeping well. It's no surprise; what did I expect? It's the mind-buzzing. It never goes away. Questions, questions, more questions. They are, perhaps, the only thing of any value that I have left. I wonder why I never discussed them with Cassandra. Perhaps she had some answers? Perhaps you do?

So answer me this: Where are all the wise men? Where have they gone? Where are our Platos, our Aristotles? What *is* going on?

When I was younger – when I was eighteen – I was full of the confidence of youth . . . yes, it's the same hoary old story, but it's true. I was young and forthright, holding court and philosophising on any and every subject that came to mind. I felt very wise when I was young, way ahead of my peers. My limited world held no surprises for me; it held no fears. Friends sought my counsel; I was a smart kid.

But then I went to university, where I discovered there were a good deal more questions than answers. This was a bigger world, a grander world, more complex by far. Here were people from unimaginable backgrounds with incomprehensible histories, each with their own host of problems and predilections, nightmares and neuroses, fears, frights and panics. They lived different lives, ate different foods, believed in different Gods. They were studying unfamiliar subjects to unknown depths. And they confronted me with hitherto unimagined questions.

Especially those studying philosophy.

No longer a big fish in a small pool, I shrank and shrivelled until I was scurrying around in the vast ocean like plankton. How did people deal with so much confusion, so much uncertainty? Most of my peers seemed either equally baffled or wholly untroubled by such notions. But there were people who knew. I could tell. Thus it was that I looked, instead, to my immediate elders.

There were a number of mature students at the university, some of whom were as old as twenty-five. It was not long before I began to look up to these aged beings who were six or seven years my senior with something approaching awed reverence. How wonderful to be twenty-five, I would think. How wise one would be at that age. People who had reached twenty-five surely had their shit together, didn't they? The extra life experience, learning, intelligence. I mean, by the time you reached that stage, you were well away. It wasn't an accident that they were called mature students. You could see it; in their manner, the way they carried themselves, their approach to the world. No doubt about it; twenty-five was it; twenty-five was the business.

I began to hang around with them; in fact, with anyone studying at the university who was older than I. I loved their company, their approach to their studies, their carefree, untroubled attitudes. Their *wisdom*. I idolised these mature students; I could still relate to them (they weren't over the hill like my folks) and yet they were, by extension, wiser. When you're twenty-five, I thought, you must know it all.

I never stopped believing it either. Until . . . Twenty-five came and went, and I realised I had been greatly mistaken. But I figured it was just a matter of degree; a quantitative error, rather than anything qualitative; right track, wrong lay-by. I still looked ahead and said: When I'm older, I'll understand. Perhaps when I'm forty I will have had sufficient experience to really be able to make sense of this senseless world. Forty-year-olds; well, they've got it taped, right? I mean, by that stage there can be very little left that you don't understand. Life, relationships, religion, war . . . it would all be clear then, wouldn't it. Wouldn't it?

I kept looking ahead, believing that wisdom came with age, automatically, like wrinkles, and that the reason the world and its ways seemed incomprehensible to me was that I was simply not old enough. It became something to look forward to; this magical moment when one attained, for some unknown reason, great wisdom.

When I met Cassandra, I was just twenty-five.

Last night I wandered around for a while, sat in a dark, sweaty bar and drank a couple of cold beers, and then headed back to the room. I didn't eat; I didn't want to. I wasn't hungry, not really.

Actually, it wasn't that. It wasn't that at all. I was starving; I could have eaten a side of beef, raw. Or a horse. Or a camel. But I didn't have so much as a sandwich. Want to know why? This should amuse you. I went hungry because I was embarrassed. Ridiculous, isn't it. Twenty-six years old and for some reason I just couldn't face sitting alone at a table to eat. I just passed by the restaurants, one after another, my stomach rumbling, my mouth drooling. They were packed, virtually all of them, crowded with locals and tourists alike, all of whom looked like they fitted, like they belonged.

I studied them and thought: these punters are regulars. They know the score, they know the menu . . . they probably even know the waiters.

I watched in light-headed agony as pretty boys in tight jeans and short-sleeved shirts escorted even prettier girls in short white dresses and low-heeled sandals along the main drag, strolling along happily, showing off their caramel tans and bright eyes, happy people out for the evening. And I watched them take their places at lively little bistros with vines hanging from the roofs and candles on the tables, where music – performed unenthusiastically on local stringed instruments by swarthy men with Zapata moustaches and embroidered waistcoats – played gently in the background. I watched them settling in amongst the friendly buzz of chatter and activity on this warm, sensual Mediterranean night, safe and secure in the knowledge that they belonged to this. They were a part of this mass of well-to-do holiday makers; even though they were thousands of miles from where they lived, they could still feel at home. And I knew that after they had finished their over-priced meals, had drunk their thick, muddy coffee and consumed one too many liqueurs, the pretty boys would escort the pretty girls back to their white-washed hotel rooms. There, on a slightly-too-hard mattress covered with freshly ironed linen sheets, they would fuck each other stupid, and pay for it the following day when they would fall asleep on the patio in the blistering midday sun and burn to a crisp. There they all were, in couples or foursomes, and there was I, alone, knowing nothing, knowing no one and . . . I watched all this with increasing agitation and just could not bring myself to walk into any of these places and sit down.

If Cassandra had wanted me to suffer, to pay a penance, then she'd certainly have been delighted to hear about all this; how I went to bed hungry, because I was too embarrassed to sit alone in a restaurant.

And the night was filled with dreams; filled to overflowing with images both sad and frightening, none of which made sense. Tell me, when you're forty, do you stop having strange dreams that don't make sense? Do you understand the world? Do you understand yourself? And if not, why not? When do we attain that precious knowledge? How long do I have to wait? Or don't you know that either?

Want to know what I learnt from all my questioning, my probing, my wondering? I learnt that when you finally reach twenty-five, you still don't know a fucking thing. That's what I learnt. Not a lot to show for seven years, is it?

Of course, when I was eighteen I made a number of fundamental errors. What I didn't realise then was that most people didn't *want* to be wise. They didn't want to know the answers (they didn't want to ask the questions). Secondly, I learnt that twenty-five-year-olds keep their sanity only by pretending that they know more than eighteen-year-olds. Say something – anything – with sufficient confidence and you'll have a wide-eyed, impressionable, enthusiastic eighteen-year-old believing that you know what you're talking about. Twenty-five-year-olds live off the gullibility of eighteen-year-olds in order to stop themselves going crazy. And forty-year-olds do the same thing to people like me. 'When you get to my age, to my time of life . . .' they say and I listen attentively, expectantly. 'Yes, yes, tell me, tell me! What happens when you get to your age?' And they tell me. And I believe them. They've got it figured out; they know the score. But of course they don't, not really. They're lying, just like everybody else. If you've just turned forty, you'll know what I'm talking about.

I envy people on their death bed; there's no one who can tell them anything any more. There's no one who can lie and say to them: 'When you reach my time of life . . .'

You know, we really should stop pretending, all of us. We should cut this crap about knowledge and wisdom and just own up that, no matter how old we get, no matter how much we learn, we're all still as baffled and bemused as that wide-eyed gullible eighteen-year-old. Come on friends, let's come clean; let's admit that we're all totally confused and we haven't got a clue. Let's come right out and profess our profound ignorance about life, the universe and everything. Let's join together as one – the philosophers, the priests, the writers, the teachers, the politicians, the scientists, the artists – and sign a Declaration of Ignorance. Let's tell it like it is. Say it loud, we're thick and proud!

Brothers and sisters, children of the world; it's time to face facts. We don't know *shit*.

We carry on. We live our lives, do our jobs, drink our drinks, eat our food and dream our lonely dreams. We tell our tales, fuck our strangers, cheat our partners, slap our kids, read our books and lie, lie, lie. And Cassandra says: 'Go. Go and don't come back,' and we go. We do what we are told. Someone is tugging our strings, planning our lives and pulling the wool over our eyes. Someone is fucking us over good and proper.

And we all know who.

8

Cassandra gave me my own room, and a desk for my typewriter.

'Now you can write in comfort,' she said. 'Just try not to make too much of a mess around the place, okay?'

I nodded uncertainly, and followed her silently as she flew down the stairs to the hallway where, arms flailing like a windmill, she gathered herself together. It was still very early in the morning, and I was not completely awake. As you know, my own regime had me leaping out of bed no earlier than the crack of noon, and here I was, upright and partially dressed (underpants, t-shirt and bags under both eyes) at *ten minutes to eight*. This would never do. I watched patiently as Cassandra fussed with her appearance in the mirror, wishing her God speed so that I could crawl back into bed. However, it soon transpired that Cassandra had other plans for me.

'By the way,' she said, adding the final touches to her impeccable appearance, 'I've left a shopping list on the kitchen table; try and get it done before I get home. You'll find Sainsburys the most convenient. I'll cook tonight . . . you haven't tasted my cooking yet, have you?'

'No . . .'

'Well, you're in for a treat. And don't forget that we're

invited to dinner at Ros and Gerald's on Friday; it isn't a formal do, but you'll need a white shirt, so make sure you've one clean. I'll be back about six-thirty; help yourself to whatever you like – you live here now, after all – but for Christsake, don't touch the drinks cabinet during the day; I don't want to come home to a drunken sot. See you.' And with that last passing comment, she disappeared out the front door in a flurry of overcoats, scarves and document cases.

Drunken sot? Sainsburys? What was all this? I gazed out the front door as Cassandra stepped into her gleaming white chariot and sped off towards Mayfair. This dawn assault on senses and sensibilities was too much for me. I dragged myself into the front room and collapsed onto the sofa, closed my eyes, and waited eagerly for sleep to overtake me.

But nothing happened. My doziness had deserted me as completely and efficiently as Cassandra had; it was eight o'clock in the morning and I was wide awake. I looked around the huge, high-ceilinged front room as if seeing it for the first time. In truth, I had barely seen it in natural light. That morning, with the sun streaming into the cavernous interior, it looked like something out of the pages of *Ideal Home*, all stripped pine and Laura Ashley. Not my taste exactly, but not threatening, either. For the first time since we had met, I had been left alone in Cassandra's home. And I had to do the shopping.

In the kitchen, on the table beside the unread Sunday papers, was the shopping list plus three twenty-pound notes. Scribbled in almost illegible scrawl was the list of groceries, plus a PS which read: 'Take a taxi back; shouldn't be more than three pounds.' I tried to recall the last time I had taken a taxi anywhere, without much luck. As for taking a taxi to go shopping, that would be yet another first in an ever growing list of new experiences courtesy of the Cassandra Foundation for Financially Embarrassed Authors. Still, I couldn't complain; at least she wasn't expecting me to haul thirty kilos of groceries home from Sainsburys on my back. Which was just as well because, if truth be told, I was absolutely knackered.

We had spent most of the weekend – when not kitting me out with a new wardrobe – in bed. I had no complaints about that; not at the time anyway. True to my expectations, released from the rigorously imposed timetable that had previously circumscribed our coupling, our sexual activities had taken on a new fervour. Knowing that I did not have to get up, get dressed and run off at a prearranged time, allowed for a more leisurely and detailed exploration of various aspects of our conjoining, and as such resulted in a less frantic, more enjoyable and certainly more interesting experience. This was especially so following the fiasco of the cocktail party, which was something of a non-event all round. We only stayed a couple of hours, during which time I was paraded around like a prize poodle and, as Cassandra had so rightly guessed, largely ignored. No one asked me any questions, so I said very little. I had three glasses of some disgusting punch-type drink that had been so thoroughly denuded of alcohol as to render it totally impotent, ate a couple of cheesy nibbles, and avoided spilling anything on my new suit. All the other guests walked around like they were participating in some exclusive fashion parade, and no one seemed to be listening to anyone else. It was all rather dull and pointless and, all in all, I was rather pleased to get back to the relative sanity of Cassandra's house.

However, now that I had been permanently installed,

I suddenly felt a little, well . . . a little odd. It didn't feel the way I had expected, not that I'd had much time to anticipate the move. The problem, as I saw it, revolved around my status, which had never really been clarified. What, exactly, was my role? Was I a house-guest? A room-mate? A visiting dignitary? Some sort of home-help? What was the extent of my duties? What rights of tenure did I have, if any?

And what the fuck was I doing here, staring at a grocery list and sixty quid of someone else's money?

More questions; just what I needed.

I decided that a hot shower would probably put a different light on the day, then opted for a spot of breakfast before braving the high street; Sainsbury could wait an hour or two.

Of course there's no Sainsbury here, not in this Godforsaken country. It didn't take me long to come to the conclusion that this is a forsaken land. Not that I'd have felt much differently about anywhere else. Reality, so I've been led to believe, is all a matter of perception; I perceive this place to be a crock of shit, so that is what it is. Simple really. I wish I'd learnt that years ago.

Here's another of those sweeping statements that I'm so fond of. We make life too complicated. Yeah, I know, you've heard that one before, too.

My paternal grandfather, for example, had a very simple approach to life. His answer to almost any problem came in the shape of a twenty-four-inch rip saw. When I was growing up amidst my marginally extended family (me, sister Heather, Mum, Dad, Grandad, Grandma) we were subjected daily to Grandad's own unique philosophy.

One example of Grandad's utilitarian yet, in my eyes,

highly superior way of coping with an uncertain world springs readily to mind. As boisterous children are wont to do, Heather and I used to chase each other all over the house. As this was a regular activity, over the weeks/months/years that we pursued each other in this way, we grew to know the house and its contents intimately. We learned the quickest ways of skirting the furniture, how to jump over obstacles without hitting our heads on protruding shelves, how to judge cornering without falling over or colliding with door jambs. We were as adept at racing around the house as any Formula One driver at Le Mans. Until, that is, the day we took delivery of the new dining-room table. Thereafter, on three separate occasions on as many days, Heather bashed her head on the corner of the table, causing her considerable pain and distress. Grandad came up with an instant solution; he sawed the corners off the table.

My parents were rendered speechless by this act of vandalism, but Heather and I were delighted. After all, it worked. And there was more.

Grandad, as he had got older, had taken to having afternoon naps. He could rarely be bothered to climb the stairs and seek out the comfort of his bed, so more often than not he would settle down on the sofa for a little doze. But he was clearly never happy about this arrangement, as he was rarely as relaxed on the sofa as he was in his own bed. Then, one day, he realised what it was that was compromising his comfort; the armrest stopped him from stretching out fully. And therein lay the solution. Out came the saw, and off came the armrest. See? Simple. And of course, the whole family remember what happened to the bed when he and Grandma had that memorable fight.

The lunatic actions of an old tosser rapidly descending

into senility, or the reasoned acts of a seasoned pragmatist?

Grandad refused to make life more complicated than it already was. In his later years he viewed life as a sort of test between himself and the world, and became increasingly conscious of his need to fulfil the Old Testament injunction to have dominion over it and all that lay therein. Most of which was easily executed with the aid of his trusty rip saw.

During that time, Grandad also sawed the legs off the television ('Gettin' a crick in me neck'), lopped several inches off the kitchen table ('You can open the door proper now') and completely restructured the grandfather clock so that it would fit in the alcove under the stairs. I lived in fear of the day Grandad would discover that the kids at school called me 'Stretch' because of my abnormal height.

There is much to be said for Grandad's approach to life; he and Cassandra would have got along well. If it doesn't fit, alter it, change it, cut it down to size. Make it fit. In time, as you've no doubt already gathered, I would be modified by the sharp edge of Cassandra's tongue.

That first week in Cassandra's house was a revelation. Cassandra left every morning for work, whilst I stayed at home. Cassandra cooked, I did the dishes. Cassandra paid the bills, I made the bed. Cassandra said 'Jump!' . . . and I leapt. We did, however, share the housework although, it must be said, I was clearly expected to contribute more than a mere fifty per cent of the effort on the implicit understanding that Cassandra spent eight, nine sometimes ten hours a day at work and could not, therefore, be expected to come home and clean up after me.

It did not take her long to instill a full set of workable and highly effective Pavlovian responses in me, some of which were so subtle that she didn't even have to ring a bell. All she had to do was look.

Cassandra had an extraordinary array of these expressions, each one unique with its own, discrete meaning. There was the 'I'm tired, fetch me a drink' look which was similar to, but different in some indefinable though essential way from, the 'I'm tired, rub my feet' look. This in turn differed in almost imperceptible ways from the 'I'm tired, massage my temples' look. There were a number of variations on the 'Don't bother me with that inconsequential clap-trap' look and a huge variety of 'Do it now and don't argue!' looks.

And then there were her 'Fuck me' looks, about which one could write an entire book.

If I had had my doubts about my 'role' in Cassandra's house on that first Monday, by Friday it was all very clear. I was the new houseboy. I hardly did any writing that week; I was too busy vacuuming the carpets and cleaning the kitchen.

Now, whilst this wasn't what I would have called an ideal situation, I didn't want to complain; Cassandra was evidently having a tough time at work – she came home late twice that week – and I thought it only sensible to show willing. After all, she had rescued me from my Turnpike Lane pigsty and, no matter how one cared to look at it, her house was pretty comfortable. I naturally assumed that this present arrangement was something of an anomaly, and that once things had settled down and routines were established, a natural division of labour would arise that was fair to all parties concerned. In the meantime I felt it incumbent upon me to be as helpful as possible.

However, there were a few matters that puzzled me, and it was while I was thus engrossed in my daily duties that I started to wonder how Cassandra had managed all this time without a cleaning lady. So, one night, when she returned from work, shortly after I had fixed her the usual gin and tonic, I asked her.

'Don't be ridiculous, William,' she said, rather testily. 'I let the maid go the day before you arrived.'

I snorted loudly and gritted my teeth. 'It's not William,' I said with all the deliberation I could muster. 'It's Bill.'

She gave me one of those stares – you know the one I mean – and then an impatient little sigh.

'Don't be ridiculous,' she said.

No, I didn't argue. What was the point? Like I said, there was never really any discussion with Cassandra. Either you did things her way or, somewhere along the line, you'd pay for it, in one way or another.

So, this is how I lived my new life. Cassandra never asked me to contribute financially towards the household. I ate more healthily, dressed better and went out more frequently than I had ever done before, all at her expense. And all she asked in return was that I keep the house clean and behave properly in company so as not to embarrass her. This was the only sticking point in our liaison, this notion that I did not know how to behave amongst the monied classes. But I let Cassandra have her way on this; if she wanted to act like a patronising, stuck-up little bitch, then that was fine with me. It didn't stop me from telling her what I thought of her, her attitudes or her acquaintances.

As for the sex thing, well, we were in complete accord on that; we did it whenever and wherever we fancied.

We rarely declined an opportunity for a quickie before breakfast, or a debauched midnight session in front of the fire. And I surrendered happily to her depraved whims for variations on a theme, regardless of whether it included raiding the fridge or dressing up. I didn't care. Cassandra could have insisted that I strip naked, stick a toothbrush up my backside and snort like a pig, and I would have obliged. And as for my particular fancies, she seemed equally accommodating. She was, without doubt, the least inhibited woman I had ever met.

She never stopped calling me feeble and pathetic of course, and I continued to abuse her for her unemotional response. All in all, we got along just fine, embroiled in our little nest, which perhaps bore more resemblance to a nest of vipers than one of love.

As the days and weeks passed it became clear that what I had taken to be an anomaly *vis à vis* the unequal distribution of household chores was, in fact, to remain very much the norm. Although I felt that *my* work was just as important, just as time-consuming and just as fatiguing as hers, I did have to admit that my labours did not put food on the table or purchase tickets to the theatre. Consequently, I decided to swallow my pride and accept what was, in reality, a *fait accompli*; Cassandra brought home the bacon . . . and I cleaned up after it.

I'm a practical chap by nature, and soon got used to the housework, devising a system whereby I could get the majority of it completed by midday so that I could spend the rest of the afternoon writing. I would send unsolicited short stories to every newspaper, magazine and periodical in England and await their rejection slips. I also started work on my first novel, working title:

The Thin End Of The Wedge, but progress on that was slow, due primarily, I think, to a complete and utter lack of ideas.

Cassandra never asked me what I did with my days, never enquired as to what I was writing, never requested to read any of my work. Not that I would have wanted her to; I had no wish to let Cassandra treat my creative outpourings in the same way as she treated me. To call me a worthless pile of shit was one thing; to abuse my writing was another thing entirely.

During those first couple of weeks I kept myself pretty much to myself. I thought about contacting Kev, Jenny and the others, but it was clear that my new arrangements were going to take some adjusting to, and I didn't want to discuss my new situation, even with close friends, until I had become accustomed to it. And, more to the point, felt sure it was more than just a flash in the pan. It wouldn't be long, I knew, before someone realised I was no longer living in Turnpike Lane, but I figured I had a month or so before anybody started worrying about where I had gone.

Besides, I didn't really have time to see anyone. Cassandra liked me to be home when she came in from work so that I could make her a gin and tonic and massage her feet, or whatever part of her body most required my caring attention. And the weekends, of course, were extremely hectic and thoroughly exhausting; having sex with Cassandra could take on the proportions of running a marathon. As a result, I lost touch for a while with those people who had previously made up (what I subsequently learnt was called) my 'support network' (and a fat lot of support most of them had been anyway). Not that any of this seemed important; not at the time anyway. After all, there were a whole bunch of new people coming into my life; Cassandra's Cronies. And a right lot they were too.

Such is how I lived my double life, my deceitful existence, as Bill Smith: scrubber extraordinaire, by day, and Doctor William Schmidt, notable writer and philosopher by night. But only on those nights when we were among the Cronies. On all other nights I was Willy Wanker, the Walking Penis, or variations on that theme.

And on some nights Cassandra didn't come home at all. Her job, she explained carefully, required her to work evenings a few times each month. Working in a hotel meant there was always a bed for her, and so on occasion she took advantage of it.

The first few times that she didn't come home, she phoned beforehand to let me know. Not until at least ten-thirty, mind, by which time it was too late for me to make other arrangements.

After a while, the phone calls stopped, and I began to realise that my evenings were given over to waiting for Cassandra to come through the door.

On one occasion, thinking, quite reasonably, that this was a slightly unfair arrangement, I asked her whether she could let me know earlier in the evening if she was going to be staying out that night. Perhaps my timing was bad, I don't know, but Cassandra went through the roof.

'Oh for fucksake William, I can't organise my life around you. I've got a job to do – a job, I might remind you, that keeps us both clothed and fed – and if I have to start informing you of my every move I'll never get anything done. I do wish you'd think sometimes instead of making these demands on me. How can you be so selfish? Can't you see how busy I am . . . ?'

I didn't mention it again.

* * *

81

Last night I slept very badly. The night was besieged again by dreams and visions; dreadful, haunting scenes. One in particular recurred several times.

In the dream, Cassandra and I are lying naked in her bed. Cassandra is running her fingernails up and down the insides of my thighs – a procedure guaranteed to produce the desired result. Just as I'm getting ready to do something about all this, I realise that my hands are trapped behind my back. I start to struggle, but cannot move them. I ask Cassandra what's going on, and she starts whispering that I mustn't worry about it, everything's okay. But everything is not okay. I can feel now that my wrists are bound by rope, thick rope that will not give at all. I look down to where Cassandra is fondling me. Her nails are painted silver, and they're glistening in the half light. She moves her hands up to cup my balls, and her fingernails feel very cold against my skin. I'm sweating heavily, pleading with her to please untie the ropes, but Cassandra just keeps whispering 'Don't worry, don't worry', but by now my throat is dry and my heartbeat is very fast, and Cassandra's fingernails are both cold and sharp, and she's digging them into my scrotum, and the pain is terrible, and I'm still struggling but I just can't move, and my throat is so dry that I can't yell, and as Cassandra clenches harder and harder I see the blood starting to spurt out from my groin, and just as Cassandra is about to yank at my balls I wake up, covered from head to toe in a thick, heavy sweat, the sound of my own screaming ringing in my ears.

After the third re-run of this foul nightmare, unaware of the time, I got out of bed, put on some clothes and sat on the patio until, some hours later, the first light of dawn crept out from behind the mountains.

It's a little worrying, don't you think?

9

The room is about twelve feet square with plain white walls and a tiled floor. Two large slatted doors lead onto the small patio. I leave these doors open when I'm in, as they allow the most light into what would otherwise be a dark and seedy chamber. Another door leads to a tiny hallway, off of which are the closet-like bathroom with its broken toilet seat and 'electrically heated shower unit'. This is such a lethal looking piece of equipment – all frayed wires and bare, heating elements – that I daren't attempt a hot shower lest I fry like a mosquito on one of those fluorescent bug-blasters you see in all the restaurants around here. There's also a kitchenette, if you can call a sink, a cupboard and a fridge the size of a portable telly by such a name. Some would think the apartment cosy; others, of a less generous disposition, might call it a cramped fucking prison cell, or a dingy, stinking little hole.

Ah, home sweet home.

And there's a desk with a broken anglepoise that never shines light where you want it. Someone has replaced a missing spring with a thick rubber band, but he might just as well have used a Band-aid for all the good it does. Every now and then (and always when I'm trying, desperately, to write some of this down) the lamp suddenly goes into a sort of spastic fit and flays around like a whirling dervish. Nearly took my eye out the last time.

Then there's a thoroughly uncomfortable chair which has been designed for (or perhaps by) some freak of nature who, by my reckoning had legs three-quarters the length of his entire body. Whatever, it's way too high for comfort. (Where are you Grandad, when I need you? Oh yeah, I forgot; dead.) And there's a lumpy old sofa that has not only had the stuffing kicked out of it but also the bracing, so it's guaranteed to fuck your back up if you sit in it for longer than half an hour.

And there's a radio. Which doesn't work. Great.

I have stocked the fridge with local delicacies, most of which look inedible (or in some instances, already eaten), and a large bowl of exotic looking fruit now sits on the table. There are oranges, bananas and grapes; the rest is quite foreign to me and, I fear, destined to sit there and rot. One especially aggressive piece, which looked not unlike an overgrown grapefruit, greeted me with a thin, acidic spurt when I dared to puncture its hide, whilst another, a big, green leathery thing, filled the room with the odours of a urinal when I cut it in half. It was like a bad joke, like everything else I've seen of this country so far. You think it's funny? Cassandra would have laughed. And Gerald and Ros; they would have found it all highly amusing. Bits of fruit that stink of piss? Right up their alley.

Of all Cassandra's Cronies, I think I can say in all honesty that Gerald and Ros were far and away the most offensive. Gerald was a barrister. Now whilst the word is not, to the best of my knowledge, a synonym for 'obnoxious, stuck up twit with no chin and a penchant

84

for little boys', in Gerald's case the definition fits to a T. As for Ros, she was the embodiment of such expressions as 'mutton dressed as lamb', 'woman of a certain age' or better still 'rampant fat tart'. She was, supposedly, a fashion designer, although the only designs of hers I ever saw were those she had on me. Ros, it seemed, was interested in only one thing: seducing her best friends' men. Although she was a singularly unattractive woman (and bore an uncommon resemblance to her husband, the Chinless Pederast, right down to the downy bum-fluff beneath the wide, flaring nostrils) she did have her own particular charms. Not the least of which was, reputedly, a willingness to give quickie blow-jobs to complete strangers, a talent which she had somehow managed to keep hidden, remarkably, from her similarly oriented husband.

Gerald and Ros loved to give extravagant dinner parties, to which they would invite half a dozen friends, solely in order to show off their expensive house and abysmal taste. Well, perhaps that wasn't the sole reason. The events gave Gerald an opportunity to get drunk in company and bore the women present with distasteful legal anecdotes whilst Ros, by no means a model of sobriety or rectitude herself, would attempt to lure the men, one at a time, into the lavatory.

And no one, apparently, so much as batted an eyelid at this behaviour.

You'll excuse me if I appear naïve. You see, it all came as rather a shock to me. Up until the day I met Gerald and Ros, I had only read about such characters. But Gerald and Ros were the Word Made Flesh; especially so in Ros's case.

It was Friday evening and having been duly fore-warned, I cleaned myself up and put on the clean white shirt as prescribed, which I set off with a bright red tie, new blue jeans and a pair of nifty loafers, all from the Cassandra Collection. Presenting myself for approval I was met with a scowl and informed that I was attending a dinner party, not a fancy dress do. The jeans, shoes and tie were replaced with rather more sober efforts. A jacket, I discovered, was considered *de rigueur* at such affairs, and I was requested to remember so in future. It was one thing, explained Cassandra, to equip a man with decent clothes; she did not want to have to dress me as well. What was the matter with me? she asked. Was I totally devoid of good taste? I smiled. Seeing as I spend half my time poking you, I said, you'd be the best judge of that. Cassandra was not amused. Prick, she cursed. Bitch, said I. We left in silence.

As if all this wasn't enough to put me on edge, as we drove to our destination Cassandra took the liberty of warning me about Ros, in her own inimitable style.

'If you touch her, encourage her or in any way flirt unnecessarily with her, I'll cut your balls off. Do you understand?'

'No,' I said. 'What on earth are you talking about?'

'Never mind. You've had your warning. Now then, straighten your tie, comb your hair, and for Godsake William, don't pick your nose at the dinner table.'

'I shall confine all digital explorations of the nostrils to the living room, I promise.'

'Don't be smart, William; it doesn't suit you. Digital explorations of any variety are strictly out of bounds tonight, and that includes our hostess. She'll try it on, too.'

'Really?' I said. This was getting interesting. 'What do I do if she grabs my plonker when handing round the hors-d'oevres?'

'Nothing. Unless, that is, you want it to end up impaled on a cocktail stick.'

That was one thing you could always count on with Cassandra; her descriptive sense was exceptionally graphic.

The house was one of those grand Edwardian jobs, full of mismatched period furniture and dreadful, gilt-framed portraits of miserable looking ancestors; at least, I presumed they were dead family members, as they all appeared equally lacking in the chin department. (But inbreeding will do that to you; accentuate physical anomalies.)

We were shown into the 'library', an over-furnished study which, despite its high ceilings still managed to feel decidedly poky; it seemed the wrong place to gather for a pre-dinner aperitif, giving a sense of neither grandeur nor comfort: just ostentation.

Fortunately we were not the first to arrive; two anonymous couples had already made themselves familiar with Ros and Gerald's drinks cabinet. I was introduced, first and foremost, to the host and wasted no time coming to a just and accurate assessment of him (I believe the shorthand term that best approximates is 'nerd'). The lady of the house stuck her head round the door briefly, apologised that she was temporarily ensconced in the kitchen and assured us she would be with us shortly. Or rather, she slurred words to this effect whilst wiping a dribble of something red and winey off her furry chin. The Famous and World Renowned Doctor Schmidt then shook hands with a Reggie and Helen Jester and a Tom and Susan Some-thingorother. Reggie and Tom were both barristers, sharing chambers with the aforementioned Gerald Doppler, QC. The wives, I regret to say, were both rather nondescript, as no doubt befits the partners of thrusting, go-ahead legal types. I believe one of them was a teacher and the other had something to do with animal cruelty, although what exactly was never made particularly clear.

Gerald leapt into what he must have thought was his 'charming host' act. In an overly expansive gesture, arms flailing like a windmill, he motioned us into the room and, taking hold of my elbow in a manner that I considered too familiar by half, asked me what my tipple was. Alas, Cassandra spied the mischievous smile that came automatically to my lips, and before I could deliver a suitably witty riposte ('the peculiar shaped thing on the end of your . . .') she had elbowed me discreetly in the ribs.

'William will have a dry sherry,' she interrupted, thus depriving me of the only decent feed line I would get all evening. With the sherry merely adding insult to the injured ribcage, the tone was thus set for the rest of the evening.

'You look as ravishing as ever, Cassandra,' said Gerald with not a trace of authenticity. I could tell he didn't mean it because he was eyeing me up and down at the time.

'Thank you Gerry; you're looking pretty smart yourself,' replied Cassandra with all the sincerity of a British Rail announcement apologising for the late arrival of the nine-fifteen to King's Cross. Did anyone see me cringe? I suspect not. Alert now to the promise of an enraptured evening filled with aliens spouting truisms, clichés and platitudes, I swiftly downed my sherry and waved my glass in Gerald's direction for a refill. Even Cassandra was starting to behave like she'd just emerged, fully formed, from a giant pod in the cellar. It was clear that there would be only one way to see this evening through, and it did not involve sobriety.

Of the other guests, Tom seemed to be very edgy. He kept looking around him as if expecting someone or something to come flying through the walls at any moment. He shuffled around, shifting his considerable bulk from one foot to the other, looking for all the world like a snotty little boy that needs desperately to take a leak but has neither the courage nor wherewithal to ask for permission to leave the room.

The other man, Reggie, was a sort of scaled down identikit version of our host, although he seemed altogether less natural, as if he had forsaken his own tics, habits and mannerisms and adopted a false yet complete set from Gerald. Within minutes he was all over Cassandra, making stupid remarks about how gorgeous she was and using any excuse to paw her. It was a little unnerving, seeing Gerald and Reggie standing side by side; that one such specimen should exist was cause for concern, but that there should be two of them broke the boundaries of good taste.

As for the women, they too seemed to congregate around Cassandra, although from what I could hear of their conversation, they must have had 'vacant' stencilled on their foreheads. Who *were* these old farts? Why were they all buzzing around Cassandra like she was queen bee? Didn't Cassandra have any normal friends? Didn't she know anyone her own age? This lot were in their early forties. At least, the men were. (Yeah, forty; don't think that *that* was lost on me, either).

After about fifteen minutes of thoroughly inconsequential chit-chat, (they really did talk about the weather) during which time I managed to help myself to a large Scotch whilst Cassandra was otherwise engaged, there was a rallying cry from the kitchen. With a little shriek of excitement, we were all beckoned to the dining room by the most impressive bust I'd ever seen.

I must apologise at this time for the rather picaresque turn of phrase and the perhaps coarse nature of this and other observations, but as a writer I've often found that, when confronted by the absurd, obscene or excessive, the best course is to 'tell it like it is', and Ros, it must be said, was surely blessed . . . doubly so. She was wearing a skimpy dress that was cut so low at the front and rose so high above the knee that all it seemed to cover was her navel. If she had sneezed boisterously, I doubt the thing would have been sufficiently robust to hold together. Well, perhaps I exaggerate, but it was clearly insufficient in both design and support for a woman of such ample proportions. Like June in the rousing song from *Carousel*, Ros was busting out all over. I watched in a sort of horrified fascination as she led the way, sidling up to the dining table as if she had something wet and wriggling caught in her knickers.

'Now then William, why don't you sit here, next to me,' said Ros, patting the chair beside her. Cassandra threw me one of her fierce 'don't mess with me, buster' looks which I chose to ignore. I could suddenly see the potential for a bit of fun. I smiled lasciviously at my hostess and took my place. Susan Wosname sat on the other side, whilst Cassandra sat directly across from me, so that I remained just within kicking distance. My shins might well come in for a battering, I thought, but I intend to enjoy every minute of this. If Cassandra insisted on dressing me up like an accountant and dragging me along to these ridiculous charades, these 'duties', then I fully intended to make the most of it.

While the maid rushed around serving soup, Gerald

struggled with a corkscrew and a bottle of expensive claret, overdoing the innuendos about always having difficulty getting it out. Everyone laughed politely while I tried not to yawn too loudly. What was the matter with these people? What were these arcane rules and regulations that insisted they behave this way? I glanced at Cassandra hoping for some sort of clue or, failing that, at least a knowing wink or nod to assure me that she knew how absurd this all was. But Cassandra was giving nothing away; no nods, taps, winks, tics, smiles, signs or signals. Just that extraordinary, glacial demeanour that made you think ... what was it? Ah yes; it made you think of the women in Grimm's fairy tales: wicked witches and ice-maidens.

It was difficult to look at her for long when she was closed-off like that. I couldn't explain why; there was something intensely hurtful about it. I had seen it a couple of times before, that haughty, self-sufficient air. It worried me. I sensed that there would be little support from Cassandra that evening and that I would have to brave these cold, uninviting waters alone. If this was a test, it wasn't a very pleasant one. Still, I had my pride; I would not let her down. If she was wondering whether or not I could behave myself properly in company, then tonight she would learn that there was more to Bill Smith than met the eye.

'So William,' came a voice from out of the blue. I looked up to see Gerald glaring at me arrogantly; it wasn't a pretty sight. 'At long last we get to meet the mysterious man in Cassandra's life?'

'Really?' I said. 'When?'

Susan Thingamy sniggered, while Cassandra drew in a deep breath. That was more like it; at least she'd reacted.

'Ah, very amusing,' laughed Gerald falsely. 'Still, we're delighted you could make it tonight. Cassandra explained all about your busy schedule. We feel most honoured.'

Quite right, I thought. Because of this dumb dinner I'm missing out on a good evening's ironing. 'Well,' I said after a suitable pause; 'I could hardly miss an opportunity to meet Cassandra's closest friends, especially after everything she's told me about you.' I smiled again and, under cover of table cloth, felt Ros lay her chubby, sweaty palm on my knee. I looked across to her and, as she smiled, smelled the reek of cheap alcohol and rotten teeth waft its way towards me. I assumed she had spent the entire evening supervising Cook in the kitchen, wooden spoon in one hand, bottle of cooking sherry in the other.

'I understand,' said Ros, pausing rather deliberately, 'that you're a writer. And yet, if you don't mind me saying so, you look so young!'

Ah yes me dear; beneath these navy dress trousers stirs a virile, twenty-five-year-old dong with, dare I say, a literary bent. Invite me to the bathroom and I'll show you my curlicues . . .

'William's one of those fortunate individuals who is destined to look young for ever; the Cliff Richard of the academic world, isn't that right, darling?' Cassandra's voice had cut through the air like a flashing sabre. I looked across and gave her a little quizzical frown but she paid no attention. I downed the claret in one and played with my glass, hoping someone would notice that it was empty.

Not that this interruption fazed Ros in the least. I felt her apply a little more pressure to my knee. Easy does it lady, I thought. And stop drooling; it can't be considered good table manners even in your own home.

'Indeed,' she said breathily, her bosom rising and falling dramatically, as if she were being pumped up by someone who had failed to notice that she had a slow leak. 'And what do you write, if you don't mind me asking?' she continued urgently, straining at the bit. Playing for time, I braved a spoonful of the soup; it was cold.

'I'm known primarily as an essayist, as I'm sure you're all aware.' I looked around me for confirmation. Everyone nodded rather seriously; I knew I was on safe ground with this lot. 'But at present I'm working on my first novel.'

Cassandra glared at me, sensing I was about to embarrass her, myself, our hostess . . . something. I felt the now familiar pressure of itinerant fingers ride up the inside of my thigh and settle on my groin. So this is how the other half behave, eh? I controlled the emergent grin rather better than the stirrings in my underpants.

'How interesting,' said Ros, giving a gentle squeeze. 'And what's it called?'

John Thomas, but then I'm sure you know that already . . .

'*The Thin End of the Wedge*,' interrupted Cassandra again, spitting out the words like watermelon pips.

For the second time in just a few minutes Cassandra had managed to intercede and draw all attention to herself. This time she even got to Ros; the hand was withdrawn rather swiftly.

'Really Ros,' continued Cassandra with barely a breath; 'this is excellent soup. Your own recipe, or did you steal it from one of your friends?' She gave a coy

93

little giggle, quite out of character; everyone else laughed too. Everyone except me.

'Honestly, Cassandra!' said Ros, refusing eye contact with her guests. Clearly I had missed the joke. If there was one. I half suspected that the laughter was less to do with anything amusing that Cassandra had said, and more to do with some sort of social code that, once again, I was not privy to. This was getting tricky. I didn't care about these people, about their stupid ways and ridiculous manners and neither did I want to be a part of it. But I did not want to feel out of my depth, and I certainly didn't want to give Cassandra the satisfaction of telling me that I had been gauche or socially unacceptable. But there was something going on here that I did not understand.

I had perceived no especial threat or menace in Cassandra's tone, and yet clearly something she had said commanded attention. It was very strange. These friends, or whatever they were, seemed to defer to Cassandra at the drop of a hat. For a moment I thought that she must have something on every one of them, some dark, tawdry secret that could allow her to hold them all to ransom in this way; 'Kiss my fanny or I dish the dirt'.

It didn't make sense. As for our hostess, for all her authority, real or alcoholically induced, she had shrunk from Cassandra's crack about the soup. She had retreated so swiftly that one couldn't help but feel sorry for her. Why hadn't she fought back with a suitably acidulous response? She must have been capable of it. What was she afraid of?

A barely noticeable but no less deathly silence descended on the gathering for just a moment or so; it was eerie and discomforting. Cassandra had done this; Cassandra had cowed these people with just a few curt words that meant nothing. I wanted to stand up there and then and tell them all to knock it off. Who did they think she was? The Queen? Lady Muck? The Chief Inspector of Police?

And in that moment, as this collection of well-to-do strangers slurped their soup in ominous silence, something that I had suspected for some time, but to which I had not really given credence, became crystal clear: I was living with a sorceress. A woman who could cast spells over assembled crowds, turn merriment into misery, celebration into chaos, who altered every event that she attended by her mere presence, disturbed whole systems just by walking into them. I know this sounds far-fetched and hysterical, but I had seen it with my own eyes on a number of occasions previously, to a lesser or greater extent, and what was happening here, around the dinner table, was just a more intense example.

And what I was seeing, of course, was charisma in action. Not the false, bloated ego-allure of film stars or certain rock musicians that passes for charisma in this era of reduced expectations. This was something else, something that had nothing to do with fame or popularity. We talk of extraordinary people, of people with charm and magnetic appeal, but we rarely meet people with power. People who exert influence over others, not by brute strength or clever words, but by some sort of innate, manipulative potential. Yet in that moment, as these so-called friends and acquaintances – surely powerful and influential people in their own right – faltered beneath Cassandra's imperious glare, I realised that this was what Cassandra possessed, and she had it in spades.

After this brief lull, conversation picked up again, although now it seemed even more artificial than before.

Gerald started in on a story about the case with which he was currently involved, concerning two notable members of a well respected London Club who had recently been caught in *flagrante delicto* in some public convenience in Knightsbridge. The other two barristers listened intently, commenting at intervals on points of law and, it seemed, morality, injecting comments which were both inane and frequently derogatory. Did people really talk about 'shirt-lifters' in this day and age? Clearly they did and, what was more worrying, these people were friends of the woman with whom I was currently living or 'shacked-up with', perhaps. Susan engaged Cassandra and Helen in a lively discussion on, of all things, bestiality, something with which her work evidently brought her into close contact. Meanwhile Ros, having emptied yet another glass of wine, partly down her extravagant *décolletage* but mostly down her throat, started wriggling again whilst explaining that any friend of Cassandra's was a friend of hers. None of this seemed like suitable table-talk to me, and if Cassandra had ever worried that I would embarrass her in front of such people, then it was truly upsetting to imagine what she must have thought of me. If this was what the 'right people' considered etiquette, then I was thankful to have been born on the other side of the tracks.

As the evening wore on I became more and more aware of two things; firstly that, despite initial attempts to be polite, no one was the least interested in me or anything I had to say. Secondly, and more disturbingly, Cassandra was grimacing at me every few minutes, throwing looks of distaste or anger in my direction. I sensed I must be doing something wrong, or rather, not doing something right. I laid into the claret with rather more verve than intended hoping Dutch courage might substitute for the real thing which, at some time during the evening had evidently taken a hike. I became so unnerved that I started to sweat a little more effusively than normal; the collar and tie were starting to constrict me, choking me, and I would have given anything to have been allowed to take them off. But, of course, it was proscribed.

Cassandra, on the other hand, looked cool, calm and collected, perfectly at home in these hideous surroundings. She also looked stunning, with her shiny black hair and Cleopatra eyes, putting to shame the other three women at the table. Even as I sat there hating her for what she was doing to me, I was also keenly aware that, once we were naked and alone, there wasn't anything I wouldn't do for her.

Before long Ros's hand had strayed to my knee once again. I tried to appear interested in what she was saying without arousing Cassandra's suspicions, but concerned as I was, and with more alcohol flowing round my bloodstream than I'd had for some time, I could not help but stare at Ros's heaving breasts now and then. My sense of discomfort was heightened by the knowledge that to ignore the hostess would appear rude, and yet to encourage her would be fatal. Cassandra had warned me before we had left the house; she had warned me about Ros. Don't pick your nose and *don't encourage Ros*. And what was I doing? Clearly, whatever it was, it was wrong. At the beginning of the evening I had thought it was all just a joke, one of Cassandra's many unamusing diversions, but just looking at her expression now, I knew otherwise.

The main course was uncooked; I cannot recall what it consisted of. By this time I was so aware of the enraged presence emanating from my partner across the table that I was unable to concentrate on anything else. I had never experienced that before; it was almost as if I felt guilty, merely by being the focus of Ros's attention. I drank another glass of wine.

Come now Cassandra, be sensible. It's hardly my fault is it? You invited me here. I have done nothing to inflame Ros's passions, and surely it would be a greater sin to ignore her. What am I supposed to do? You can't be jealous. Just because I'm looking at her amazing tits. Surely you don't care about me, do you? I'm just your bit of fluff, aren't I? Your post-feminist, reconstructed toy-boy. Nothing serious, nothing *real*. And please, stop making me feel like I've done something wrong. I haven't . . . I haven't done anything. Please Cassandra, stop *looking* at me that way.

I was becoming more confused by the minute. On one hand, part of me was pleased to see Cassandra so worked up over nothing; it was as if I needed to believe I could inspire jealousy in her. On the other hand I was scared; scared of getting it wrong, scared that she would misinterpret my behaviour, scared of letting her down. It was ridiculous, and I know now that much of my fear was alcohol-induced – I'm a paranoiac drinker – but it was no less real for that.

Seeing Cassandra, seeing her expression, the way she was handling herself, the way she appeared . . . it suddenly dawned on me how important she had become to me. We had only been seeing each other for a short while, and I had been living with her for less than a week, but already Cassandra had taken on a significance in my life to which no other woman had come close. Perhaps in the light of what I've already told you about our relationship, this sounds strange or even unlikely. But remember, here was an attractive, intelligent, worldly woman who had not only taken an interest in me but had literally hauled me out of what was, in truth, no better than the gutter. She had fed me, clothed me, put a flashy roof over my head. More to the point, within the sexual arena she had done things with me, to me and for me that no other woman had done. She had made my dirty dreams come true. And she had initiated most of it. There were times with Cassandra when I was out of my mind with pleasure. There may not have been any love, or indeed any affection on her part, but as far as I was concerned, Cassandra was the most extraordinary woman I had ever met, and suddenly the thought of being without her filled me with a sort of dread. For all my ranting and raving and insistence that I be consulted on this and that, I had already decided, following the cocktail party fiasco, that if I had to play silly games in order to appease her, so be it. It was a small price to pay in order to stay with her, to live with her, to have her. The problem was, although I was prepared to play the games, I hadn't realised how complex the rules were, how many tricks and turns there were. I hadn't realised, in fact, just how dangerous it all was.

I looked across at Cassandra and caught that steely gaze; I felt like a little boy who had been brought before the headmistress, charged with misbehaving in class. I took another drink. The conversations around me had become more animated and the guests, no doubt spurred on by the wine, had become altogether more boisterous. Ros, now much the worse for drink, had lost interest in me altogether and was busy flirting outrageously with Tom, whilst Gerald, wholly oblivious to this, was trying to strike up a conversation with me across the table. Cassandra just looked on.

Suddenly, all I wanted was to impress her; I wanted her to feel proud of me. I wanted to be a reflection of Cassandra's merit, her quality, her uniqueness. I wanted to be *right*.

These thoughts left me paralysed; someone threw another question at me, and I fumbled, having not heard it in its entirety. All the time, Cassandra just sat there, watching. That steely gaze penetrated deep into the heart of me, and an icy chill shot down my spine. It was becoming increasingly difficult to concentrate on what was going on around me. Unable to amuse these people, or hold court with my tales as I had done so successfully at Jenny's dinner parties, I began to shrink into myself. Worried, then, that the others might think me a bore or, worse still, an idiot, I attempted to make good with useless smalltalk, over-compensating like crazy and giving credence to the very impression I had sought to avoid. Cassandra said virtually nothing. She neither seconded nor denounced my pronouncements, as if I were a complete stranger whom she had met for the first time that evening, and would probably never see again. I knew then that I was in trouble. For all my posturing and independence, I *was* out of my depth with these people. I was flapping and flailing for all I was worth, but the truth was, I was drowning; I was drowning in my attempt to impress. I was doing it all for her, for Cassandra's sake, and yet, seeing me struggle, she would not reach out a hand to help me, and the more I struggled, the further away she seemed. And, what's more, there was just the trace of a smile on her lips, a cruel smile, as if she enjoyed seeing me squirm.

More confused than ever, I would have done anything

to elicit a friendly gesture from her, some sign of recognition, something, just so that the others could see that she cared about me. So that *I* could see that she cared about me. But there was nothing; she was as cold and calculating at that dinner table as she was in bed. And as I contemplated the truth of this, I started to feel a little unsteady, a little sick, and I realised that, in reality, I meant nothing to her. I was just her straight-man, her house-boy, her pet; I was Shrivelling Willy, Willy Wanker, Doctor William Schmidt. I was Cassandra's Clown.

10

That was the start of it, I guess. Up until that evening I hadn't really given a monkey's about Cassandra in any terms other than as a bedmate. At least, that's what I believed. Or rather, that's what I had been telling myself. True, I was living with her and, to all appearances, it may have seemed like I was being kept by her, but I saw this as a purely practical matter; as Cassandra had said, it wasn't convenient having me living so far away and besides, there was plenty of room in her house. It did not, to my mind, change the status or nature of the relationship.

As regards her paying all the bills, I considered this fair exchange for the work I did around the house. It wasn't as if I cost much to keep; in fact, I'm sure I was a cheaper option than the maid who had performed some of my duties prior to my arrival. As far as I was concerned, Cassandra was getting excellent value for her money and had no reason to complain. I'd have bet that her previous home-help wouldn't have given Cassandra a 'special massage' at three in the morning, nor serve her breakfast-in-bed at weekends dressed in nothing but a straw hat and a G-string.

It was a fundamentally reciprocal arrangement, and I too got what I wanted, on a regular basis, and without any of that soppy nonsense that usually gets in the way. Cassandra and I had a wholly acceptable working arrangement with no strings (other than the aforementioned undergarment) attached. It was perfect.

So why was I suddenly at sixes and sevens whenever Cassandra left for work in the morning, or phoned to say she wouldn't be back that night? Why did I think about her all day instead of getting down to writing?

And why did I panic at the thought that, at any moment, Cassandra was going to turn around and tell me to leave?

My God; it was almost as if I was in love with her, or something equally ridiculous.

It's raining now; bloody typical. Just as I start to think the only decent thing about this place is the weather, it starts to piss down. Let me tell you, sub-tropical downpours do nothing for this place. Except sweep all the shit and garbage into the streets and flood the pavements. Not that I want to go out or anything. But even so, it didn't have to rain.

And there's another thing. I thought I saw someone spying on me this afternoon. I know that's ridiculous, but there was this funny looking geezer in a raincoat (must have been a local, eh?) walking around outside the apartment, and he had a pair of binoculars around his neck and every now and then I saw him aiming them at the building and peering through them. I considered going out there and asking him what he was up to, only I didn't want to draw attention to myself. Besides, I don't speak the language, and the last thing I needed was some sort of commotion. He was only there for a few minutes, and for all I know he could have been a bird-spotter or the local Peeping Tom. Still, it didn't make me feel any better.

Mind you, what would?

Men treat women like dogs. Sweeping statement number three, if I'm not mistaken. I don't think they do it out of malice or anything; they just can't tell the difference. (Kevin, my oldest mate, is particularly incapable of making the distinction, judging from the sort of women he has cavorted with over the years, ha ha. Little joke for all those unreconstructed sexist pigs out there). No, what I mean is, men have no real idea of how to interact with the opposite sex. The main problem is that men do not see women as being human. Women are strange, alien beings who bear a passing resemblance to blokes (two ears, two eyes, walk upright on two legs) but don't actually behave like real human beings (i.e. best mates, Clint Eastwood, Frank Bruno) at all. Women are either pets or possessions, sparring partners or house-maids, prostitutes or cooks. Business women are threatening, intelligent women are frigid, independent women are butch, beautiful women are cock-teasers and ugly women are, of course, dogs. But they're never just women, and they are certainly not equal, equivalent or in any way as valuable as other men. In fact, received wisdom holds that women are only good for one thing, and even then not as good as a vivid imagination and your own right hand.

Is it any wonder we've got problems?

Men are threatened from the moment of their conception by the very *idea* of women. Women brought them into the world, fed them, dressed them, wiped their bums and walked them to school. Women comforted them when they fell and scraped their knees, and protected them from angry drunken fathers who couldn't communicate with the women in *their* lives. Let's face it, for your average macho-type male with thick biceps and big hairy balls, this is not an auspicious start in life. And as he grows up, women will continue to be the primary controlling factor in his life. Once he reaches adolescence (and from then to eternity), in the eyes of his (male) peers, his status and desirability will depend upon who he 'pulls'; his reputation upon how many he beds; his success on how well he marries.

How can a man be admired, upheld, respected when his entire existence depends upon women? There is only one answer; women must be shown to be a good deal less important than they really are. Man must rise above women somehow. Women must be minimised, degraded, belittled. Man must have dominion over women in the same way as he, supposedly, rules the Earth and all that abides therein.

And up until recent times, in places as divorced and distinct as Fulham and Fiji, by virtue of a winning combination of ignorance; insensitivity and brute strength, he has achieved this much to his own satisfaction. Indeed, to such a degree that he has become incapable of distinguishing women from the rest of the animal kingdom.

But, of course, he can never get away from the fact that he *needs* women. In fact, he literally cannot survive without them. Hence he treats them like he treats his best friend: the dog. Dogs are indulged; they are provided for, warmed with affection, taken for walks. Dogs are stroked and petted and given little treats now and then. They are also house-trained. And they don't talk back. Of course, if they fail to behave properly, they are admonished. If they snap, bite or fail to remember their place, they may well be put down.

It strikes me that men do a lot of that; putting women down.

No, I'm not making any special claims for myself. I'm not about to pretend that I'm any better than the rest of them. I've made my mistakes too; I've behaved as abominably as the next man and maintained a supreme, self-satisfied ignorance about my actions, defending myself to the last. But at least I've recognised it. At least I've admitted that I'm guilty.

Sort of.

That evening with Gerald and Ros left me winded and, I have to say, emotionally bewildered. For several days I wandered around the house like . . . I don't know, like someone who has recently suffered a bereavement but can't remember who it is that died. Cassandra didn't seem to notice, or if she did, said nothing. Not that I expected any sign of concern from her; if I had ever had any doubts about the depth of Cassandra's care for me previously, then following that fateful dinner party, such doubts had disappeared swiftly and completely. Whatever Cassandra's feelings for me, they did not then, nor would they ever, include concern for my wellbeing. This was something I had to assimilate and understand, and the quicker I learned it, the better. There was no point deluding myself that it would ever be any other way. And after all, wasn't that what I wanted? No concern, no caring, no commitment; nothing to get in the way of an otherwise thoroughly healthy relationship?

Who was I kidding? It may have started that way, but already things were starting to change, if not for her, then certainly for me. Yes, she could be rude, dismissive and hurtful and, yes, she frequently treated me like shit, like I didn't matter. But the fact was, I was *there*, living with her, in her home. She *wanted* me there, even if it was only for sex and vacuum cleaning. Here was this amazing woman who looked gorgeous, had a fabulous body, and was just about as intelligent a person as I had ever met, and she was looking after me. In fact, perverse as it may sound (and even though I had lived with a woman once before) I felt more 'cared for' than I had since leaving my parents' home seven years earlier. The truth was, I was growing very fond of Cassandra in more than just physical ways.

About a week after the Gerald and Ros débâcle, it occurred to me that part of the problem (that is, *my* problem) was that I felt too isolated. Hampstead wasn't my manor; I knew no one there except for Cassandra and I had not yet had any opportunity to meet anyone new. More to the point, I hadn't made any contact with my friends for ages. It occurred to me that I might just be suffering from a sort of delayed homesickness; with all the excitement of moving, it hadn't registered that there might be things that I actually missed.

It was also true that I couldn't keep my present where-abouts secret for much longer; I suspected that Jenny and Kevin had both tried to contact me and that if I didn't touch base soon they'd start to worry. Besides, at some point they'd all have to know about Cassandra. Now that I had made the move to her place, regardless of how Cassandra or I viewed the arrangement, pretending that this was no longer 'serious' would not cut ice with the likes of Kevin; you could never pull the wool over his eyes.

In addition, I felt it was about time that Cassandra met some real people. I had had to put up with some of her dreadful associates on two separate occasions and would no doubt have more to suffer before long. That Cassandra mixed with these types at all was a worrying notion; that they seemed to be her only contacts was terrifying. No, enough was enough; Cassandra would have an opportunity to meet *my* friends on *my* turf and, what's more, she'd learn a thing or two about normal, fun, unpretentious folk for whom friendship was not measured in status, style or pounds sterling.

Consequently, having checked that we were not 'booked', I arranged to meet Kevin and his then girl-friend, Mandy, at The Merry Fiddlers for a few drinks one Friday night. I told them I'd be bringing a friend, and that Kevin was to be on his best behaviour.

And then I told Cassandra.

'Not a chance.'

'What?'

'It's out of the question.'

'Oh come on, Cassandra; I had to put up with Mister Pederast and The Suckling Pig for an entire evening. All I want you to do is meet a couple of friends of mine.'

'What, for a couple of pints and a game of darts? Well really William, it's very kind of you to invite me, but I don't think it's quite my scene . . .'

'I want them to meet you; it would mean a lot to me.'

'Too bad. I'm afraid I have far more important things to do than hang around one of your seedy dives talking to some brainless bimbo while you get legless with some East End oik . . .'

'For Godsake Cassandra, don't be such a prig.'

'Prig? My, that's an unusual word . . . but then I forget, you're a writer, aren't you. No doubt all that slumming around gives you inspiration. I'm sure it must

108

be wonderful to garner so much first-hand experience about low-lifes . . .'

'You're talking about my closest friends.'

'Exactly.'

'You stupid bitch . . .'

'Oh do fuck off, William. Whatever makes you think I have the least interest in meeting your drinking buddy and his bit of spare?'

'Then do it for me?'

'Don't be ridiculous.'

'My God, you really don't give a shit, do you?'

'It isn't in the contract, William; it isn't part of the deal. And incidentally, did you remember to pick up my clothes from the cleaners . . . ?'

What could I do? She was right, of course; it wasn't part of the deal. She was not required to meet my friends, nor attend any social gatherings of mine. She was a busy, working woman. Her time was precious, her spare time was her own. And although it was never said, it was not difficult to infer the rather obvious corollary to all this; if I didn't like it, I could lump it/stick it up my arse/leave (delete as applicable).

But I thought – I mean, I had hoped – that she might just see her way to indulging me, just once.

More fool me.

Kevin gave me a hard time when I cancelled on him; I gave him some feeble excuse about Cassandra having to work late, but he saw right through that one.

'So we're not good enough for her, eh Bill?'

'No, no, nothing like that . . . you've got it all wrong. She has a very demanding job, Kev; really. She just can't make it. I mean, she often comes back late; sometimes she doesn't come home at all.'

'Oh yeah?'

'Yes . . . what . . . what are you getting at?'

'Getting at?'

'Come on Kev, I can hear it in your voice.'

'Nah, it's nothing. Sounds like quite a character, this Cash-in-handra. Popular girl is she?'

'What's that supposed to mean? Come on, spit it out. What are you trying to say?'

'Whoa boy! It's not for me to say anything, unless I'm asked, of course.'

'Okay, I'm asking,' I said, perhaps a bit too impatiently. It wasn't like Kev to be cagey about anything, and I felt a little unnerved by his attitude.

'Look, there's no need to get upset. Just do me a favour; watch yourself, okay?'

'What are you talking about? Who have you been talking to?'

'I ain't been talking to no one . . . why so defensive?'

'I'm not being defensive . . . I just . . . look, it's difficult to talk about over the phone. This thing with Cassandra; it's just . . . different, that's all.'

I heard Kevin clear his throat and then sniff loudly; I knew there was more that he wanted to say, but for some reason he was holding back.

'Yeah, well,' he continued after a moment; 'like I said, be careful. Just make sure you're not getting screwed over. I know you Billy-boy; you can be a right bloody softie sometimes; I've seen women walk all over you in the past . . .'

'Bollocks . . .'

'Yeah? You forget how long I've known you. Just watch your step, eh pal?'

'It's not a problem, Kev.'

'If you say so.'

'What is it with you? What's brought all this on?'

There followed one of those long, uncomfortable telephone silences. I could hear Kevin sighing at the other end; it was most out of character.

'Look Bill, I know you're not the most conventional bloke in the world, but you've been acting really funny lately . . . even for you. You haven't rung no one, you haven't come out for a beer, you move in with this woman from God knows where at the drop of a hat, you don't leave no forwarding address, and we ain't seen hide nor hair of you since.'

'I know, I know . . . I should have been in touch earlier. I'm sorry. But it's just been really busy. You know how it is sometimes.'

'Yeah, well, if you ask me, this posh bird has got you by the short'n'curlies . . .'

'Wrong!' I blurted out, a little too emphatically. 'But only 'cause she's shaved them off,' I said quickly, hoping to cover my anxiety. It was a feeble joke, meant to diffuse the whole situation, but it didn't work. Kevin laughed, out of politeness I suspect. Or perhaps pity. Either way, I didn't want to discuss it any more right then, not with Kevin, not with anyone. 'Look Kev, give me a break, huh? So she's a bit . . . unusual. It just needs a bit of time, okay?'

'Whatever you say, Bill. Still, I'd like to meet any woman that can keep you away from the pub for six weeks on the trot.'

'Yeah, well . . .'

'See you around then.'

'Sure.'

Of course, I never did persuade Cassandra to meet Kevin and Mandy, and besides, within a week he had traded Mandy in for a new model. But that's the way it is with Kev; never get hung up on a woman, never say 'I love you', and never become dependent on them.

He must have thought I was fucking crazy.

11

I finally started work on *The Thin End of the Wedge*, only to find myself suffering once again from the dreaded Writer's Block. Anyone who has ever attempted to write a novel will know how frustrating this is when they're half-way through a potential masterpiece. In my case, what made it all the more frustrating was that I had only written four pages. Previously, as you know, I had stuck to a strict programme of sitting at my type-writer every day, come what may. Now that I was ensconced in Cassandra's house, the necessity for such a rigid schedule had somewhat lessened. In the past I had forced myself to commit something to paper in the per-haps erroneous belief that the act – which I considered magical anyway – would somehow keep the wolf from the door, regardless of whether or not I produced any-thing that was saleable. But where are the wolves in Hampstead? And is it necessary to undergo such an austere regimen just to keep the occasional spaniel from running up the garden path?

Consequently, relieved of having to keep life and limb together in the immediate future, I made the fatal error of assuming that, thus released, my inspiration would be free to wander, and that with that freedom, it would somehow grow and mature. It would then descend upon me, perhaps at less regular intervals, but with no less fervour, and breathe greatness into my work. As a result, I needn't worry if I missed the occasional day slogging it out on the keys.

So I abandoned my daily sessions at the desk and, instead, began to fill my afternoons with all manner of interesting new occupations, most of which were designed to fill the time waiting for the Muse to arrive. And the first thing I did was learn to cook.

I have to admit that having never had anything other than a consumer's interest in food, I had remained untroubled by culinary expertise of even the most elementary kind. Don't get me wrong; I loved eating good food. However, for myself, I had rarely managed to rustle up the enthusiasm to fix anything more demanding than scrambled eggs on toast. Not that I actively disliked cooking; it was just not high on a list of priorities that included, to my mind, much more important endeavours (like sleeping, drinking and watching television).

However, on the odd occasion when I had acted as Cook's Assistant, I had thoroughly enjoyed the experience. Being an assistant meant, of course, that I had no real responsibilities, which rather let me off the hook as far as the success or otherwise of the meal was concerned. Consequently I was an enthusiastic worker, willing to perform even the most menial of tasks as there would almost certainly be some novelty value associated with them.

On those rare occasions when, at the command of one girlfriend or another, I had been summoned to lend a hand for some forthcoming event, I was not particularly interested in the inventive aspects of cooking, such as creating new and wondrous dishes, or indeed the aesthetic or artistic factors associated with presentation. These were matters way above my head and best left to the experts. No, I derived the greatest pleasure from those most mundane aspects of preparation: peeling and chopping.

I know this must seem odd; these, after all, are the very jobs that most cooks despise for being dull and laborious, the necessary evils of the vocation. But for someone who lives for the most part inside his own head and is rarely involved in anything of a physical, practical or tactile nature, just the act of slicing crisp raw vegetables can be immensely satisfying. There is a certain mindless delight in the simple repetitive actions that is both calming and therapeutic. It is refreshingly undemanding. The same goes for peeling; potatoes and carrots being particularly gratifying. That the ultimate result of these efforts is in itself pleasurable rather than merely functional only adds to the enjoyment. I discovered that I could quite happily spend several hours thus employed. Provided, of course, that I wasn't called on to carry out these tasks more than, say, once every three months.

As for actually taking charge and producing a whole meal however, that was out of the question.

So it was that I came, like a virgin, to the great arena of the culinary arts. And I started where, no doubt, many a tyro cook begins his or her apprenticeship; with cookery books.

As Cassandra had once boasted, she was no mean cook herself, although, if truth be told, since I had become a permanent fixture in Cassandra's home we had eaten chilled, ready prepared meals from the likes of Sainsbury and Marks and Spencer more often than not. Still, she possessed an impressive array of cookery books

– an entire shelf full – covering everything from *Japanese Vegetarian Dishes* to *A Hundred and One Ways with a Marrow* – a book which, even with my limited experience, did not seem intended for serious gourmets. None the less, prior to diving head first into this new and exciting venture, I spent many a happy hour leafing through the more colourful volumes, reading recipes and committing certain fundamental procedures to memory so that, when the day came, I would not have to stop midway through cooking, say, a lasagne in order to look up how to make a bechamel sauce. It was all very educational and reminded me, more than anything, of my school days in the chemistry lab, weighing exact quantities of this to make solutions of that to add to a heated mixture of the other. I knew it couldn't be quite that simple but I was a reasonably confident sort of bloke and felt that, with sufficient practice, I would soon excel at my new project.

As one might have expected, Cassandra had a kitchen equipped with every sort of modern device. Being something of a consumerist freak, you could just about guarantee that if you could plug it in, Cassandra had one – or maybe two. Foodprocessor, mixer, electronic scales, fan-assisted oven, microwave, volcanic lava-grill . . . you name it, Cassandra had it. Frankly, I didn't much care for any of the fancy gadgets. As a newcomer to the game, it seemed only to complicate matters. Ignorant though I may have been when it came to the finer aspects of culinary grace, it struck me that, apart from an oven and a couple of gas rings, all you really needed were the ingredients, a few pots and pans, a good chopping board and a few decent utensils. Consequently, of all the equipment that Cassandra had installed in the kitchen, to my mind the most impressive

116

(and certainly the most useful) gadgets were a set of Sabatier knives. These knives, balanced like precision instruments, were razor sharp and so clean, so accurate in their cut, that I felt certain that, if caught short, a qualified surgeon could use them to whip out someone's appendix.

The knives were also to provide my first important lesson; the kitchen, like any work environment, can be very dangerous if not treated with respect. So it was that I discovered that, whilst it is to some extent true that it is the blunt knife that cuts you, it is the sharp one that mutilates. This I learned to my cost when I nearly took off my thumb whilst slicing an onion. Cooking, it seemed, was not an occupation to be taken lightly by the faint-hearted or, in my case, the cack-handed.

Much to my delight, I soon discovered a latent talent for preparing meals which were both aesthetically pleasing and, if I say so myself, rather delicious, and although Cassandra seemed singularly unimpressed by my efforts, I gained a great deal of satisfaction from it. As I did from knitting.

I know what you're going to say, but just before you do, think for a moment; apart from the sexual stereotyping that, so engrained in our culture, insists that knitting is a solely female activity, why shouldn't a man derive equal pleasure from creating something practical and beautiful out of wool as he does, say, out of wood? I'm serious. Admittedly, one is fighting a few hundred years of commonly accepted typecasting here, but look at it from my point of view. There I was, a creative, artistic individual, looking for new ways to express that creativity during a short lull when, to coin a phrase, words had failed me. Being open-minded and prepared to try anything once, it was only a matter of time before

I began experimenting with activities that were not just new to me, but which I would not, under normal circumstances, have ever thought of trying. One shouldn't be limited by sociopolitically imposed expectations . . .

Actually, to tell the truth, it was Cassandra who suggested it. It was only an off the cuff remark, I'm sure, but since I'd stopped smoking (at Cassandra's insistence; well, it was her house), I had become extremely fidgety. Cassandra suggested I take up knitting as something to do with my hands. I remember, clearly, my first response.

'Fuck off . . . what do you think I am?'

'A real man,' said Cassandra sarcastically. 'You know, for a supposed writer, you can be quite a little reactionary. I thought your "art" was all about self-discovery. You're not even prepared to challenge some extremely petty gender definitions. What's the problem, William? Scared someone's going to call you a sissy?'

'Oh come on Cassandra; how many men do you know who knit?'

'Ever heard of Kaffe Fassett?'

'The place on Hampstead High Street that does the brilliant cappuccino?'

'Dolt. Kaffe Fassett is probably the leading knitwear exponent in the world. And what's more, he looks like a god; I know a number of women who would drop their knickers for him any day.'

'What, in exchange for some hand-knitted bloomers perhaps?'

'Really William, I'm astonished at your response. Anyone would think I was suggesting you take up crossdressing.'

'But why on earth would you want me to take up knitting?'

'I don't want you to do anything. I couldn't give a shit; you can take up hang-gliding for all I care. It's just incredibly frustrating seeing you spend every evening fiddling with bits of paper and tooth picks.'

'It's withdrawal.'

'I'd have thought you'd be an expert at that.'

'Oh very funny.'

'I'm just trying to be helpful. I realise that you're going through a set of readily acknowledged responses – I understand most drug addicts have similar reactions – which is why I was suggesting something different, something practical. You could put all that nervous energy into making something, creating something. And you wouldn't even have to stop watching that precious telly of yours. That way you'd have something other than fresh breath and twenty extra years of life to show for your efforts . . .'

I knew, of course, that whenever Cassandra started in on something like this, there would be no end to it until I capitulated, which is the initial reason I agreed to try knitting: anything to get her off my back. As it turned out, she was right. And, to my great surprise, she even gave me a few lessons. Every evening for a week we sat down together, I with my needles primed, ready, if not eager, to be initiated into this most feminine of household pursuits.

Before long I had learned such manoeuvres as casting on, casting off, knitting plain, knitting purl, tensioning the wool so as not to drop stitches (then learning how to pick up if, horror of horror, I did drop a stitch) increasing, decreasing and, of course, how to read a knitting pattern. It didn't take me long to master the basics and, more importantly, it kept my hands and fingers occupied during those long hours in front of the television when I would otherwise have worked my way through half a packet of Silk Cut. In fact, as the weeks passed, I began to get quite proficient.

Thus it was that, during the weeks that followed, I sublimated my creative drives in cooking, knitting and other pursuits that I would not have previously associated with men. As I was already responsible for cleaning the house, washing the dishes and buying the groceries, it all fell together quite naturally. I had become a househusband. All we needed now were kids . . .

Time began to pass more slowly. I found I was a good deal more tired than I used to be, that I lacked some of my usual energy and enthusiasm, but I didn't let it concern me. And I didn't let on to Cassandra that I was finding things less than ideal, as whenever I even mentioned that I was tired or fed up, I'd find myself on the end of a tirade about how hard she worked and the hours she put in and how tired she was. Mind you, I had to hand it to her; as tired as she was after a long day at the office, she always found the energy for sex. It was a phenomenon. In fact, to be honest, her demands were, I thought, a trifle unfair. Whereas we had started off on very much an equal footing, I was no longer *always* in the mood for some heavy petting in the early hours of the morning, or a quick bunk-up before breakfast. Where she found the stamina for all this bumping and grinding was anyone's guess; I think she must have had a hormone imbalance of some kind.

I had avoided contacting Kevin again, as I knew he could not possibly understand the arrangement I had found myself in. Not that I fully understood it myself. I knew that something extraordinary had happened, but could not put my finger on the crux of it. Somewhere along the line I had begun to realise that my previous notions of sexual and gender identity were rather simplistic, lacking in any real insight. Perhaps I would never have been prepared to adopt my new role had it not been for the unusual nature of my everyday existence. As a writer, I had always believed that I was a little more open-minded than most of my acquaintances, which was why I was frequently drawn to new and different experiences.

I had always loved exploring concepts like change, especially when it concerned environment, behaviour and belief. If I had not been so poverty stricken since leaving university, I would certainly have travelled more extensively. And, what's more, I would have been prepared to go out on a limb. To me, it was what being a writer was all about; Cassandra had really pushed the right button when she accused me of being reactionary because I had recoiled from the thought of knitting. To be a writer was to go beyond such things. Even if that meant discomfort. Or embarrassment. Or isolation.

And, despite my reservations concerning this setup with Cassandra, now that I was entrenched in this brave new world, I could not help but think that it was, in some way, doing me good. It was, after all, a new experience of strange and dramatic proportions. So what if I allowed Cassandra to bully me now and then, to dictate what I wore and how I behaved? And what if this meant re-examining the traditional roles adopted by most men and women involved in sexual relationships? Wasn't this important to the life of the artist, struggling to come to terms with such concepts as identity, self and meaning?

And what did it matter if, as a result of all this, I was miserable most of the time?

These were matters that I knew would be beyond Kevin, so there seemed little point in even discussing them with him. For Kev, the world was pretty much black and white; men were men, women were women, and each had their clearly defined roles and responsibilities, and as far as he was concerned, any deviation from the *status quo* was tantamount to tampering with nature. In fact, when it came down to it, there was nobody with whom I could discuss any of the doubts that lingered in my everyday consciousness; doubts about the sense of what I was doing, the potential harm it might be causing.

Mind you, there was always Jenny, but for some reason, I just didn't want to discuss it with her. It wasn't that I couldn't trust her; on the contrary, apart from Kev, no one was closer to me. And I'm sure that, as a woman, she would have made some interesting observations concerning my predicament. Which is probably why, in the end, I didn't contact her either. Perhaps I was scared of what she might say. Maybe I was worried she'd tell me something I didn't want to hear. Something I knew to be true.

Cassandra continued to work late, sometimes three nights a week, and by the end of the month I had already become bored with my daily round of housework. This should have occasioned one of those wondrous spurts of creativity; boredom plus plenty of free time usually does wonders for the aspiring novelist. However, the Muse was still out to lunch.

Having tired, temporarily, of knitting (following the completion of a quite splendid sweater) and with little else to occupy me, I took to watching daytime television. It started by accident; I'd turn on to BBC to watch the one o'clock news and, more out of *ennui* than curiosity, I'd stay tuned and watch whatever followed. And whatever followed that. And I discovered a hitherto unknown trait in my character. I was a junkie, and my poison was soap-opera.

This was definitely a turn-up for the books. I had long ago rejected the notion that I was an intellectual snob (in an age when the deconstructionists had somehow reduced all art to the same level). Nevertheless, I still maintained that in order for a television programme to engage me, it had to possess a certain quality that could be critically analysed as such, the sort of quality, say, that sets William Golding apart from Harold Robbins. I knew Cassandra abhorred soap-opera, situation comedies and game shows, believing that they traded in the lowest common denominators and pandered to morons; it was one of the few matters on which we agreed. However, with my newly acquired lethargic disposition, I soon began to look forward to one-thirty on Tuesdays when I could catch up with the exploits of a certain Australian community who were all suffering from terminal ham-acting. I never shopped on Wednesday afternoons for fear of missing an episode of the thrilling series about the everyday lives of doctors and nurses who worked in the strange hospital where none of the patients ever recovered (as evidenced by their regular weekly re-appearance), and Thursday was a bumper day with two half-hourly soaps which were quite indistinguishable from each other.

And against the Orders of the Establishment, I would raid the drinks cabinet for a small Scotch to supplement the visual sedative to which I was becoming addicted at an ever increasing rate.

The typewriter lay dormant for three months. Dust gathered on the keys. Desire had joined the Muse for a holiday, and I became firmly ensconced in the rituals of my day-to-day existence. I considered writing a book about the life and times of a male housewife: *A Day in the Life of Doctor William Schmidt: Domestic Operative*. But I couldn't be bothered.

Besides, when would I have had the time?

12

Today I saw a ghost. At least, that's what it felt like. The ridiculous thing is, I don't believe in ghosts, spooks, spirits, elves, goblins, imps or bogeymen. I don't believe in other people's myths. Still, whatever it was, it was enough to put the frighteners on me.

It all started when I went out for a walk this morning. This loss of sleep is beginning to get to me, but so too is being cooped up inside this cramped little shit-hole. So, even though I was so tired that I kept bumping into things, I figured I'd better get out, or else I'd probably crack up completely (if I haven't already done so; after all, who's to say? There's no one I know here to tell me if I'm acting strangely, no way of gauging my behaviour. For all I know, I could be acting like a madman).

I waited until about ten o'clock and then headed out into the streets. I remember looking around me as I locked the door; it sounds crazy, but I had the strangest feeling that someone was watching me. I wondered whether I might catch a glimpse of that guy with the binoculars, but he was nowhere to be seen. Still, I didn't feel comfortable, although this could, of course, have been because I was suffering from severe sleep deprivation as well as advanced paranoia. Yeah, go on; laugh. I would.

I headed towards the main street and then walked around aimlessly for about half an hour, sticking to the shadows and trying not to look too out of place. The town was gearing up for business again, like it did every morning about this time; it seemed late in the day to get started, but then again, there was no one else about, so I guess the shopkeepers knew what they were doing. Knowing that virtually every other foreigner in town was probably tucked up in bed, fast asleep following some late night rave or other didn't do much to improve my mood. Strange that; how everyone here was having a good time except me. It occurred to me that, once upon a time, I used to have good times too, although for the life of me, I couldn't remember when; it seemed like such a long time ago,

Everything was so quiet and peaceful, it was a little eerie. The place felt like a ghost town, in complete contrast to its night-time incarnation. I wasn't happy wandering around, so after a while, what with the sun already beating down and making me dozy and thirsty, I ducked into this funny little café just to find some shade and, for the first time since I had arrived in this stinky little town, did not feel like dashing straight out onto the street again.

It was one of those cosy-but-drab Mediterranean style places, stuck in a basement, down a side alley off the main street. Not the sort of place you're likely to bump into holiday makers, although it did have an English menu scrawled onto a blackboard behind the bar, just in case.

It was very dismally lit inside, which was probably why I didn't feel so conspicuous there. I waited for my eyes to adjust to the darkness, then descended the few stone steps that led down from the street. Save for two small tables near the door which benefited from a few rays of light from outside, the place was mostly illuminated by dim yellow bulbs. These twenty-watt globes, barely brighter than candles, dangled naked and dusty from the plaster ceiling, while others, stuck in decaying, tassled lampshades, hung motionless above the tables.

Two miserable-looking, olive-skinned waiters were slouched up against the counter, looking almost as tired as I felt. They just stood there, smoking cigarettes and chatting half-heartedly in their guttural and totally incomprehensible language. But I didn't have to speak the language to know that these two clowns would rather be elsewhere, doing something else; anything else. When they finally got moving, they made every attempt at service look like the Tasks of Hercules.

A rusty, three-bladed fan, like something from another era, turned slowly in the centre of the ceiling, wafting damp, fusty air through the café. As it clattered away, the exposed metal blades cast strange rotational shadows onto the cracked plaster ceiling, which metamorphosed swiftly from one silhouette to another, like an animated Rorschach blot.

The place was furnished mostly with splintering cane chairs and rickety wooden tables that, like everything else in there, had once seen better days. I walked inside and sat down at a small table by a wall. It occurred to me that the café resembled, more than anything, a dilapidated version of Rick's Café Americain from *Casablanca*, which may have been why I felt reasonably comfortable there, *Casablanca* being just about my favourite film. In fact, it was kind of disappointing that there was no Sam sitting at the piano playing 'As Time Goes By' – as apposite a song as I could have imagined at that precise moment.

I'd managed to pick up a three-day-old copy of an English newspaper from one of the mini-markets on the main street, but it was too dark inside the café to read it comfortably, so I moved to one of the tables by the door where I could at least differentiate the black type from the white newsprint. I ordered a coffee and began scouring the pages for . . . well, let's just say I became pretty heavily engrossed in it. When the waiter finally brought my drink across, I looked up and noticed that another figure, a woman, had appeared next to the counter. For a moment I paid no attention; as I said, it was pretty dark in the café, and as the woman was standing in shadow, I couldn't really see too much in the way of detail.

But then, just as I was about to return to the newspaper, she stepped forward into the light from one of those hanging bulbs, and my heart exploded in my chest. It was all I could do to stop myself crying out.

A cold, clammy sweat broke out instantaneously across my forehead, and my stomach heaved and churned, as if some maniac had just thrust a mincing machine into my guts. I was sure I was going to throw up, and put my hands to my mouth in case. The waiter stared at me, evidently troubled, although I suspect this was more to do with the thought of me making a mess than any real concern for my state of health.

I continued to stare, horrified, at the woman; she had turned her head away now, but I didn't dare take my eyes off her. What was going on? Was this some sort of joke, some dirty trick? Was someone playing games with me, or was I seeing someone who wasn't really there?

Of course, I knew that it *couldn't* be Cassandra, even if she did have the same build, the same black hair, same dress style, but even so the resemblance was startling. No, more than that, it was terrifying.

The waiter was standing over me, looking somewhat puzzled. Not that I could blame him. I forced a smile and made gestures to the effect that I was okay. This took rather more effort than I wanted to expend just then, but eventually the man shrugged and wandered back to the counter. The woman – whoever she was – had moved out of sight; I presumed she was sitting around the corner. I reached for the coffee, hoping that a shot of caffeine would stabilise me, but as I lifted the cup my hand, still shaking alarmingly, ensured that the hot black liquid merely shifted location, from cup to saucer and thence to floor. I replaced it on the table before I scalded myself.

Now, I know that in circumstances of extreme stress, the mind is prone to play tricks on you, but even accepting that I was the victim of some sort of hallucination did not make me feel any easier. If anything, it only made me more nervous, adding to the tension and highlighting the danger I was in. Up until that moment, for all my supposed fears and concerns, it hadn't really registered just how precarious my situation was. I really shouldn't be hanging around a major city, even if it was in a foreign country; it wasn't good for me, wasn't good for my already frayed nerves. I decided that it was time to make a move, the sooner the better. I'd have to go somewhere less crowded, somewhere off the beaten track; somewhere where ghosts couldn't find me.

I kept my eyes trained on the spot where I'd seen Cassandra's phantom *doppelgänger*, but she didn't make a re-appearance. I was tempted to stand up and wander around the side of the counter just to check, but I wasn't feeling all that brave and besides, it would have looked suspicious. And after my near-fainting fit, I didn't want to attract any further attention to myself. I could tell that the two swarthy waiters were discussing me anyway. I sat there for several minutes, not doing anything, just staring at the counter, until the thumping in my chest and the pounding in my head had subsided.

I folded up the newspaper and, rising slowly to check my balance, dug around in my pockets for some money. I left a big tip; I figured that would keep them happy. My hands had stopped shaking so I grabbed the cup; the coffee had cooled so I downed the contents and, trying not to hurry, turned and walked up the steps and back into the street.

And then I ran all the way back to the apartment.

There had been a number of women in my life before Cassandra. Wendy – the last woman for whom I had had any real feelings – had also ended up making my life a misery, albeit for different reasons. Or were they? Like Cassandra, Wendy had been one of those women with a forthright character and well developed sense of self, but she didn't take over my life in the way that Cassandra did; at least, not in so calculated and blatant a manner.

Wendy was a very *able* young woman; she was several years my junior but quite mature none the less. She was Personal Assistant for some advertising big-wig in Covent Garden, a position of which she was clearly proud. Frankly, I never did figure out the difference between Personal Assistant and Stepped-all-over-secretary-cum-general-dogsbody. Still, Wendy seemed happy enough in her work – she wasn't particularly ambitious. In fact, she wasn't particularly bright to my mind, and even though this was to be a contributing factor when we eventually split, during most of the time we were together, it didn't seem to matter at all. Why? Because Wendy loved me. At least, she said she did, and her actions only seemed to confirm it.

No, I don't really know what love is. In my occasional search for metaphors and similes (the province, I realise, of poets and dreamers, but that needn't exclude aspiring novelists, right?) I have usually shied away from such simplistic notions of comparing love to the natural world: my love was never like a red red rose, nor like a fervent fire; if anything, when it came to the elements and the natural world, I always saw love as closest to the wind: something invisible in itself, but frequently devastating in its effects.

But I could tell that Wendy loved me, not just because she said so, but because of the way she treated me. She realised soon after meeting me just how single-minded I was about my writing, and never allowed this to interfere in any way in her affections for me. Most of the other women who had shared my life, even if it was only for a short while, had looked upon my literary aspirations as some sort of hobby, and would become quite irate whenever my writing took precedence over them. One in particular – her name was Sarah, I think – used to refer to the typewriter as the 'other woman', and told me that if only I spent as much time caressing her as I did the typewriter, we'd probably have a half-decent relationship.

But Wendy never saw my writing as a problem, nor did she see herself as having to compete with it for my time or attention, and I honestly believe, even now, that she wanted, more than anything, for me to be a successful novelist. I don't think this had anything to do with faith; I don't think she ever actually *believed* I would be successful. But when you love someone, you want them to achieve that which is most important to them. You want them to be happy.

It really couldn't be simpler.

But Wendy wasn't a fool. She knew that money was a problem, that I didn't have a 'career', that I had no intention of finding one. And yet, knowing all that, she was not only prepared to get involved with me, she even helped support me while I was getting started. Wendy was nothing if not generous.

The relationship took off like a rocket. It was very much a case of right time, right place. We were both single, unentangled and, I guess, looking for love. I knew as early as our first date that this would be more than just a flash in the pan; not because there was any-thing extraordinary about our first evening together, but for the opposite reasons. There was something very natural, very easy about being with Wendy; there was no need to play the sort of games that had previously been so much a part of my courting rituals. Wendy was happy to be with me, did not want to play hard-to-get, or pretend that she was anything other than what she appeared to be.

It soon became clear that we were made for each other. We enjoyed the same food, had similar tastes in music, and laughed at the same television programmes. We felt the same way about the Church, modern art, and wine that came in screw-top bottles. And, more importantly, we enjoyed being in each other's company.

Within a few weeks of getting to know each other I had moved into her flat. There didn't seem to be much discussion about it; it was just considered the right thing to do. And besides (as she pointed out at the time), it would help save on the rent.

I know what you're thinking; there's a pattern emerging here, right? Well, perhaps. But living with Wendy was a completely different experience to living with Cassandra. For a start, I wasn't totally dependent on Wendy. I helped pay the rent and the bills; we shared the costs of food, drink, electricity, heating . . . everything was split down the middle. This isn't to say that it was a completely equal arrangement; Wendy earned more money than I did as a rule, and consequently she was the one who treated when we went out to a movie or for a meal. She used to insist, in fact, that she pay. She never made me feel bad about it, or even indebted to her. As far as she was concerned, it was the only way; after all, she had money, and I didn't. She was very pragmatic that way. And trusting. If the roles had been reversed, she used to say, then I'd be treating her. With Wendy, everything was black and white; it was, I recall, an extremely refreshing attitude.

We lived together for the best part of a year. I had a part-time job working in a second-hand-record shop three days a week. I didn't mind the work at all, even if it was a little dull. But it really didn't bother me; it wasn't the least taxing and it meant that, intellectually and creatively, I remained fresh and unburdened, and still had four days each week to pursue my writing. Short of manual labour (the thought of which horrified me) it was probably the best way I could have found to earn a few quid on a regular basis.

Our life was a pretty simple affair. We stayed at home a good deal and watched television; we went to the pub every Friday with Kev and the crowd for a few drinks, and there were enough parties at the weekends to ensure we didn't cut ourselves off from other people and new influences.

Once every few weeks we'd shoot off to the

133

countryside for a couple of days, usually to Kent or Sussex, and hole up in some quaint bed and breakfast with a few bottles of wine. We even went to Brighton for a Traditional Dirty Weekend which, although fun, was probably no dirtier than any other weekend. But (and this the main point of all this) it was fun. Wendy and I got along very well. Sex was good, if not particularly dynamic, tending, as a rule, towards the familiar and guaranteed rather than the adventurous and risky, and in general we found little to argue about.

All sounds rather idyllic, eh? The perfect romance, right? So what was the problem? Why did it all end?

Simple really. I hate to say it, but I'm afraid it's true. The whole thing became dreadfully dull. We fell so naturally, so easily into a sort of suburban mediocrity that we began to resemble one of those couples you see in terrible TV sitcoms. One day it suddenly dawned on me that, unless there was change (probably of a serious and dramatic kind) the relationship would soon stifle me. I imagined waking up one morning to find myself penned in by all the accoutrements of a safe, middle-class marriage; mortgage, children and regular trips to the nearest DIY centre. That was it; that was when I knew something would have to change.

But there were no such doubts in Wendy's mind; no questions, no confusions. Wendy wasn't much interested in change; she was happy with everything just as it was. She had no ambition to speak of, beyond getting her annual rise and pushing for a few days extra holiday. She had no desire to make the world a better place (or worse place or different place or *anything*), no reason to believe any of that had anything to do with her. Such things were the domain of politicians, freedom-fighters, charity workers and perhaps, just perhaps, novelists and

134

poets. But it certainly wasn't the business of personal assistants or, indeed, anyone who worked in the advertising industry.

Because of Wendy's simplistic world view, she was actually the stronger personality. Wendy possessed a certain solidity and strength, an inexorable conviction concerning what she believed. She was never baffled or befuddled, particularly when it came to matters moral or political. Like I said, everything was black and white with Wendy; I never heard her say that she couldn't make up her mind about something, or had difficulty making a decision. Nor was she ever confused over which side to take in any confrontation. And if anything proved too complicated to understand on first examination, it was dismissed as being irrelevant.

And, ironically, because of this unwavering system of belief, Wendy was able to dominate me very easily. Which may have been why I had not resisted any of her moves, from our first kiss (her instigation), to moving in with her. She believed life was a simple affair, made complicated only by people who insisted on being equivocal or ambivalent. There was good and bad, hot and cold, right and wrong. Simple. And so whenever I started to philosophise or eulogise or even just equivocate on some matter or other, Wendy would react by insisting that I was worrying about nothing or else taking things too seriously.

About eight months into the relationship, Wendy started dropping hints about buying a place together. She never nagged me to get a 'proper' job, but I sensed that, deep down, for all her support, she was hoping that I would eventually let the writing take a back seat and apply myself to some sort of career. Not that she ever said this in so many words. But there were plenty of intimations and suggestions. I knew then that it was just a matter of time before marriage and babies appeared on the agenda.

In the end, I suppose the main problem was that it was all too easy. There were no fireworks, no sparks ... none of those things that make relationships fizz, none of the energy that makes being in love something exciting, something to write home about ... or even something to write about, period. It was, in a word, pedestrian. Because Wendy was no Brain of Britain, after a while conversation became fairly mundane. It hadn't mattered at the start of our affair (what does?) but as time passed it began to irritate me. She always claimed that one day I would be a great writer, but frankly, she didn't know what great writing was. Because she loved me she told me that everything I did was wonderful, but this meant nothing really. Wendy's taste ran more to pot-boilers than the sort of literary fiction that I, in what may well have been a delusion of grand proportions, aspired to, so I never felt her critical appraisal of my work particularly valid.

All in all, Wendy was a good kid with a heart of gold. She was popular, friendly and good natured, and would have done anything for me. And I threw it all away because there were no fireworks. As Kev said just after we split up, what I needed wasn't another woman but a bleeding shrink, because someone who would give up a good woman like Wendy needed his head examined.

The break-up was awful. There were tears, plenty of them, but none of them from me. There were a number of heated conversations, and a good deal of emotional discussion; lots of why-why-why and what-did-I-do-wrong, but throughout it all I remained curiously detached. I couldn't even get that upset. All I knew was that it was wrong, that it had to end, and that it would be better for both of us if we went our separate ways. It sounds terribly heartless, but that wasn't how I saw it at the time; I just thought I was doing the right thing. In retrospect I see that my behaviour was pretty callous. I think my actions must have hurt her terribly but, for some reason, whilst I had never wanted to cause her any pain, I somehow didn't really care. I knew there was something odd, something a bit disturbing about this, how I was able to cut myself off emotionally from someone who I had once cared for so much, but it was not the right time to question my motivation. I just kept justifying my conduct by saying that there was no point in two people staying together if one of them doesn't want to be there; it was no good for either party. In an odd way I thought I was doing her a favour.

Three months later I was drowning in an agony of self-pity. Not only was I lonely and miserable, but I suddenly saw what I had done, what I had given up. I tried calling Wendy a couple of times but, quite understandably, she wanted nothing to do with me, and all I was left with was a sense of my own stupidity. And the refrain from Joni Mitchell's 'Big Yellow Taxi' – one of our favourite songs – playing over and over in my head like a record that's stuck in the groove: '*don't it always seem to go, that you don't know what you've got till it's gone . . .*'

Having made that mistake once, I swore I'd never do it again. But of course, no two situations are ever the same, no more than any two people are the same, and although more than a year had passed, I suspect I was still suffering from this state of self-condemnation when Cassandra burst in on my life.

* * *

Within two months of moving in with Cassandra, my daily routine was well established. Although I was now hitting the bottle with regularity each afternoon, I made sure that I was always sober by the evening, just in case Cassandra deigned to grace me with her presence. She was spending more and more time at work, and her long absences from the house were beginning to distress me. I wasn't sure why I was so bothered by this; after all, it wasn't as if I was unused to spending long periods alone. Truth to tell, I was starting to feel a little lonely, stuck in that great big house of hers all day, every day, while Cassandra was out hobnobbing with the rich and famous, or whatever it was she did all day. In the end, I think it was simply that I missed her.

Part of the difficulty in all this was that I was beginning to become dissatisfied with the emotional content of our relationship, or to be more accurate, the lack of any emotional content. I wanted us to become closer – after all, Cassandra had become the biggest influence in my life, the most important person for many years – and it was clear that there was no way we would become more intimate if we never spent any time together other than when making love. I was still upset over what had happened that night at Ros and Gerald's, how helpless I had felt, how much I seemed to want – to need, even – Cassandra's approval. I hoped that if Cassandra could see me as more than just a bed partner, then her attitude towards me might change.

The problem was – as I could tell by my increasingly dependent behaviour – that I seemed to have less and less to offer her. I sensed that I was in danger of losing her simply by becoming a bore and a drudge. The thought that I might be repulsing Cassandra through these sins of omission played heavily upon my mind. I would have to find ways to endear myself to her once again; after all, she had clearly found me of sufficient interest and appeal to install me in her house in the first place, so surely it was just a matter of re-igniting that initial attraction.

I came up with a plan, one which I thought was guaranteed to succeed. Even if Cassandra wasn't the least interested in how I filled my days, there was no reason why I should act with equal indifference when it came to her other life. Perhaps all she wanted was for me to show some curiosity in the one thing that, above all other things (me included) was of importance to her: her work.

Cassandra didn't talk a great deal about what she did during the day; all I knew was that she was some high-powered PR person at one of Park Lane's five-star hotels. From the start there had been a sort of unspoken rule that we would not delve into each other's work, although why this should be the case had, in itself, never been questioned. I had half suspected that it was because, after a long day dealing with other people, the last thing Cassandra wanted was to hear about my literary struggles, about the exhausting search for the perfect sentence, or the trials and tribulations exacted upon the creative spirit by the much loathed yet all-powerful Writer's Block. Fine. This was one area where no reciprocity was required; I would merely start showing a casual interest in her career, and perhaps I would benefit not only from being seen to show such selfless concern, but also through getting to know her better. After all, Cassandra was, above all else, a career woman; perhaps the clues to what made her tick lay in the nature of her work. Either way, it was worth a go because, let's face it, when it came down to brass tacks, I didn't really understand Cassandra at all.

The experiment was short lived. After three days Cassandra turned on me, and with her usual clarity explained just where we stood *vis-à-vis* discussing her work.

It just so happened that, for the previous week or two, I couldn't help but notice that, as soon as Cassandra arrived home, before she had even kicked off her shoes or ordered her gin and tonic, she had headed straight for the bedroom. I often heard her shuffling about in there, opening drawers and slamming them shut. Naturally, after a few days, I began to wonder what this was all about, so one evening, just after she stormed in through the front door, I followed her at a discreet distance up the stairs to the bedroom and watched her from the hallway. I wasn't spying – at least, I didn't see it that way – I was just curious. After all, it wasn't as if she had strictly forbidden me to follow her up the stairs when she arrived home after a hard day's work.

As it was, there was nothing the least revealing about her actions; all she was doing was transferring a sheaf of papers – mostly typewritten sheets, I think – from her briefcase to the bottom drawer of her dressing table. Nothing wrong in that, or of especial interest, save for one detail. As soon as the operation was complete, she slammed the drawer shut and locked it. I couldn't imagine what sort of papers were so important or confidential that she needed to lock them away in her own home, but I knew better than to question her directly on the matter. Still, the event lodged in my mind, all the more so for becoming a regular activity.

This all coincided with my intention to find out more about Cassandra's work. I began by simply asking her about her day with a little more concern than I had showed previously. This elicited little extra information, so after a couple of days, I turned up the heat a little. Had she met anyone interesting? Was she involved in any special events at the moment? Cassandra seemed unwilling to open up, but I suspected this might have been merely force of habit. So I persevered.

On the third day, she let me have it.

'For Godsake William, I do wish you'd stop prying all the time. To be frank, what I do with my day is really none of your business. If you can't find enough in your own life to keep you occupied, I suggest you take up another hobby. Isn't there some crocheting you can do or something?'

'Sorry . . . I was just showing an interest. Nothing wrong in that, is there?'

'It's irritating. I don't feel inclined to fill you in on every minute of my day, okay? I don't have to report to you; you're not my boss. Now stop being such a pest and get me another G and T; I'm parched . . .'

My heart sank. It's a dreadful cliché, I know, but Cassandra was beautiful even when she was angry. 'Fair enough,' I muttered. I was tempted, for a moment, to ask her about the 'top secret' papers that had to be locked away in a drawer, but thought better of it. If she wasn't prepared to share even the most mundane details of her daily tasks, then I couldn't see her coming clean about the mysterious papers.

The failure of this little ruse to do anything other than aggravate Cassandra even more threw me into a dreadful depression, one which was made all the more trying as I had to hide my misery from her lest she accuse me of . . . well, what did it matter? You'd have thought from the way she went on about it that everything I did was calculated to annoy her, which couldn't have been further from the truth. Perhaps I was simply trying too hard? Perhaps if I just left well alone, then things might change. After all, there's nothing more aggravating than someone trying to please you when all you want is a little solitude.

But how would I do it? How could I leave Cassandra alone? She was all I thought about . . . well, almost. I knew it wouldn't be easy.

I tried easing off for a few days. I'd still bring Cassandra her drink and massage her feet when she returned from work, but as soon as she was relaxed, I'd go off to the typewriter and make it appear that I was busily engrossed in my own work. Needless to say, this didn't work either. Cassandra accused me of being selfish and ignoring her. What was the matter with me? How could I be so ungrateful? After all, it wasn't as if she was asking much – a little company, a little indulgence after a long day. What was wrong? Wasn't she worth it?

It was an elementary case of 'damned if you do, damned if you don't' and, correct me if I'm wrong, but I don't believe anyone has ever found a solution to this particular dilemma.

All this effort and worry soon began to take its toll on me. I was sleeping badly and my nerves started to fray. In fact, I became quite jumpy, especially when Cassandra came home. What's more, I developed a slight case of eczema; my elbows, of all things, became scaly and itchy. Although there is no absolute proof that eczema is a psychosomatic disorder, there is a body of thought that suggests such conditions are aggravated by psychological stress. I had certainly never suffered from it previously.

So, caught between the devil and the deep blue sea, I

bided my time as best I could, assuming, for some reason, that whatever difficulties existed at present, they were merely temporary and that in time things would improve. Ah, hope springs eternal.

As Kev would have said if he could only have seen me; I was in a right fucking state.

13

It is generally thought that you can tell a good deal about a person from where they live. A casual study of the location, size and type of home, along with a quick assessment of the furnishings, fittings and fixtures will probably give a pretty good idea of the owner's income, status and personal taste. A slightly more detailed look at the books that line the shelves, the pictures on the wall and, perhaps, the cassettes and compact discs lined up beside the hi-fi, all give indications to the personality and, indeed, the psychology of the master or mistress of the house. Cassandra's plush Hampstead home with its stripped pine and Laura Ashley fabrics screamed 'Yuppie!' at anyone who came in through the door. The books that lined her shelves, however, told a somewhat different story.

One afternoon, suffering from what felt like terminal boredom, I decided to amuse myself with a study of Cassandra's reading list. In all the time that I had been living there, save for perusing the cookery books, I had not so much as glanced at most of these bookshelves, which is odd, since it is often the first thing I will do when left alone in someone's living room for the first time. Actually, it is *always* the first thing I will do when left alone in someone's living room.

It's probably nonsense, but I like to think I can gauge someone's intellect (as well as their interests) if left alone with their book collection for five or ten minutes. It has been suggested to me in the past that there is something rather prurient about these investigations, and that despite its seemingly respectable intent, rifling through someone's book collection is no more intellectually rigorous an activity than rummaging through their drawers in the belief that one can divine the details of someone's sexual activity from the range and variety of their underwear. I naturally reject this comparison and the accusations of indecency that accompany it, although there is, I confess, the whiff of elitism about this exercise; I only have to catch a glimpse of a certain bestselling novelist-cum-political-also-ran for the owner to be despatched to the seventh circle of Hell, unlikely even to make it onto the Christmas card list.

These inspections are not foolproof, of course; I've been amazed at the sort of books some of my supposedly intelligent friends read. Jenny, for example, has a first-class honours degree in the History of Art, and a penchant for trashy romances, which strike me as being, from a literary standpoint, less demanding than most comic books. When I questioned her about it, she looked vaguely shocked, as if I had been prying into her sexual activities. Then she told me off for being an intellectual snob.

I wasn't sure what I would find on Cassandra's shelves (other than the cookery books that had, more or less, been my sole reading matter since I had been installed). And I have to admit that I was quite surprised to discover, nestling in between the various studies on Public Relations and Hotel Management, a fairly catholic

145

selection of what *I* defined as decent literature. Mind you, I can't imagine why I was surprised; Cassandra gave the impression of being not just well-read, but somehow encyclopaedic in her knowledge. It was only to be expected that she had read – perhaps even devoured – the works of many of the great novelists of the last few hundred years.

The books that lined her shelves were almost exclusively paperbacks, which may have been why I had barely noticed them. If there had been any hardbacks then I suspect my sixth sense for first editions (which, whilst dormant, was still relatively acute) would probably have been alerted in the hope of finding a valuable classic. But there were no such gems amongst Cassandra's collection, although it proved, on examination, to be an interesting – and, I thought, revealing – selection.

Hardy and George Eliot featured prominently, with well-thumbed copies of their entire works pitched up one end, a bulwark, perhaps, against invasions by gangs of lesser mortals. The Russians were represented by copies of *Anna Karenina*, *Fathers and Sons* and *Crime and Punishment*. There was some Zola, Balzac and an unread Flaubert, although *Madame Bovary* was clearly a favourite, its spine bent and crippled as if it had been in a particularly nasty accident. Kafka's *The Trial* sat uneasily beside Alain-Fournier's *Le Grand Meulnes*, and there was further discordance on the next shelf with *A Farewell to Arms* nestling beside *A Portrait of the Artist as a Young Man*. Sharing the same space were some rather more contemporary works, including John Fowles' *The Collector* and *The Magus* (both of which had passages marked, and footnotes added in Cassandra's hand), and some Iris Murdoch, William Golding and Evelyn Waugh.

With so much classic literature in her collection, it was therefore something of a shock for me to find an entire shelf dedicated to works by authors I'd barely heard of: Marilyn French, Dale Spender, Mary Daly, Betty Friedan, Kate Millett. The only name here that rang a bell of any kind was Germaine Greer. There were also a few textbooks on Jungian psychology, a couple of self-help manuals about assertiveness and getting what you want, and one book by someone called Andrea Dworkin that seemed, on cursory examination, to propose universal castration as a solution to the world's ills.

I couldn't understand what possessed Cassandra to read this sort of stuff. Not that I had actually read any of these 'women's' books, but I could make a good guess at the basic tenets. In truth, I hadn't had much truck with feminism down the years and I couldn't imagine that a woman as independently minded as Cassandra would be the least interested in what I suspected were nothing but the woolly-headed ravings of a bunch of over-wrought women. Still, the evidence was there for all to see.

In among these tomes there was, however, one book that caught my eye, a novel which purported to be a feminist science-fiction novel. Having never heard of such a thing before and, perhaps more crucially, having nothing else to do with myself, I sat down that afternoon and, having skimmed the first few pages, found myself inexplicably drawn into it.

Now, whilst one cannot live in any part of the developed world in this, the late part of the twentieth century and remain oblivious to the changes that have occurred in the standing and roles of women in contemporary Western society, I don't suppose for one moment that I had ever considered feminism to be a subject worth serious attention. It was, as far as I knew, all to do with women's rights, or something like that, and most of the women I had known had never expressed beliefs that they were in any way downtrodden, victimised or hard done by because they were women. Wendy, certainly, had appeared as a prime example of how self-assured and competent women could not only survive in the modern world, but actually manipulate it to their best advantage. And although I never thought Wendy to be an especially intelligent individual, I had never thought of women as being in any way less intelligent or able than men. Which is perhaps why (on the rare occasions that the subject had raised its head) I had seen feminists in much the way that the popular press had portrayed them, as weirdo extremists, beating their breasts and making a lot of fuss about nothing.

Tell me, how many men do you know who think differently? I won't even begin to tell you what my best mate Kev had to say about feminists. The fact is, for men anyway, feminism is pretty much a closed book. It doesn't affect us (even if it should). In fact, I'd go so far as to say that most men haven't the foggiest idea of what feminists are on about. And I'm sure the feminists would agree with me.

But for myself, this unusual novel was just about to change all that. Not that the book – an engrossing and well written fable that had, at its core, a feminist vision of a Utopian society – was to bring about any revelations itself. But it did get me thinking. It was the first novel I had ever read that highlighted the essential differences between the way men and women saw the world. It seemed strange that I had read women novelists in abundance and yet had never come across this other world view before. A vision that somehow showed up the deficiencies of the rational, logical methodology by which I – and evidently the rest of mankind (lower case) – had examined and interpreted reality.

I didn't really enjoy the novel; it disturbed me, pinpointing what appeared to be a huge gap in my understanding. I suddenly felt not only slightly ill at ease, but also a bit embarrassed. I had always prided myself on my insight and understanding of human nature, something that I felt was of integral importance to a writer, especially a novelist. But here was a body of thought about which I was not only entirely ignorant but also, or so it was suggested, partly responsible for suppressing.

Even more disturbing was the nature of the author's vision; an ideal society which was so foreign to me that it might just as well have been written by an alien from another world. Was this *really* how women thought and felt, how they saw the world or, more pertinently, would like to see the world? I was completely out of my depth here. Intellectually, there was much to applaud and admire but I could relate to very little on an emotional level.

Finishing the book was a very strange experience; I was, at once, both fascinated and disturbed. It was evident that there was much I didn't understand and, ever inquisitive (and despite some tentative misgivings), I went on to read a number of the more academic texts that graced Cassandra's shelves. I started with a book whose title attracted me: *The Reluctant Feminist*.

During the week that followed I underwent a highly intensive crash course in feminism, from the suffragettes to Greenham Common and beyond. It was a week in which I learned that feminism was much more than equal pay for women and more crèches in the workplace.

But what started as a purely intellectual exercise did not stay that way for long; indeed, some of the things I learned made me feel very uncomfortable. In particular, I felt quite distressed by the assertion – right at the heart of much feminist theory – that men were almost exclusively to blame for most of the planet's ills; everything from depletion of the ozone layer to warfare. It's obvious really. But what I hadn't understood was that it wasn't *human* nature that was to blame, say, for the millions of brutal deaths that had occurred as a result of war through the millennia, but *masculine* nature. And that *feminine* nature was something intrinsically different. In fact, the more I read, the more I came to see that men had been responsible, not just for keeping women suppressed and controlled, but for eliminating the feminine from almost all areas of decision making, from the political process downwards.

Even the language, I discovered, was a man-made device which, in many ways, excluded and denigrated women just by its construction and vocabulary. I started to understand why some feminists kicked up such a fuss about things which previously had seemed daft to me. I had never understood, for example, what the big deal was about substituting say, the word 'Chairperson' for 'Chairman'; after all, it was just a word, just a handy expression. But of course, to some women, it didn't look that way at all. If something as basic and intrinsic as the language gave men prominence or advantage, then where else might one find discrimination, favouritism, partiality, bias, prejudice, inequality, unfairness and chauvinism?

I continued to read. And the more I read, the more I understood. And the more I understood, the more guilty I felt.

Within a week, a picture was beginning to take shape. If I had failed to increase my understanding of Cassandra through inquiring about her work, then I was, I thought, certainly succeeding in gaining an insight through her reading matter. I did not, of course, discuss any of my emerging theories with her, as I felt certain she would consider this a further intrusion on her privacy. But I started to piece together a good deal of information about this extraordinary woman's motivations. I began to see Cassandra in a slightly different light, as not just a self-centred, self-motivated, highly ambitious individual, but a political animal, anxious to improve conditions not just for herself, but for all her kind, someone trying to get ahead not just for her own sake, but for the sake of a principle . . .

Ladies and Gentlemen, do you see where this was taking me? Such is the fate of the lovesick fool. For as a result of my newly acquired insights, Cassandra had added yet another string to her brightly coloured bow in the guise of The Noble Cause. It was, if you like, the final nail in the coffin. What's more, I now understood why Cassandra was always so impatient with me. I was, after all, just another ignorant man, a member of the species who were, according to much of the literature that I went on to read, the root cause of women's subjugation throughout the millennia. And rather than lecture me, rather than resort to the didactic, this wonderful woman was prepared to tolerate my ignorance.

I was deeply humbled.

And you can imagine the effect *that* had on my already faltering self-esteem.

This place is definitely making me nervous. I paid a special visit to the bus station today to check the cost

151

and times of buses heading south. A big mistake. The bus station was chaotic. No, worse than that; it was a huge convention of madmen and nutters, crammed together in an asylum too small by half. Hundreds of people milling around inside what was no better than a giant cattle shed, bumping and jostling, shouting and screaming, all seemingly without purpose, without design. The stench of stale sweat and urine that emanated from this hustling crowd mingled unpleasantly with the other, supposedly less offensive odours of oil and spice that mushroomed in steamy clouds above the dozens of food stalls interspersed throughout the station. It was enough to make you gag.

The midday sun had bleached the outside landscape like an over developed photograph, but little light penetrated the seedy, ill-lit booking hall, and it took several minutes for my eyes to adjust to the darkness. After stumbling around for a while like a man struck blind, I eventually found what I took to be an enquiries counter and, ever the gentlemanly Englishman abroad, took my place in a queue which did not move for the best part of half an hour. It was only when my temper started to fray that I realised my good manners were defeating me and that, further along the queue, all sorts of unscrupulous characters were butting in ahead of me. That was all I needed to see. Taking to the native customs like a fish to water, I girded the proverbial loins and, with that quiet but dangerous desperation that you usually see only in the eyes of the truly psychotic, I stalked to the front of the line and, using elbows and a few guttural expressions of my own, found a new place in the queue rather closer to the enquiries window.

It was at about this time that I became aware of a couple of extremely suspicious blokes standing by the tea stall. What drew my attention to them was the fact that they were a) white, and thus not native, and b) that they were doing their best to avoid being noticed – and making a right cock-up of it, too. That they were not tourists was evident from their clothes and strained behaviour. I tried to ignore them and put my discomfort down to the heat, the crowds and, of course, paranoia. But I couldn't stop myself from glancing at them now and then, and it wasn't until I had reached the front of the queue that I noticed they had gone.

I checked costs and timing with the man behind the counter and, with the information at my fingertips, left the bus station feeling much relieved.

However, when I caught sight of them half an hour later, wandering down a nearby street, I knew something was up. Who were these men? What were they doing here? Were they following me? If so, how did they find me? And more to the point, what was I going to do now?

I stayed in the apartment all afternoon, pacing up and down, feeling sure that the game was up, that I had been found out, traced, followed to this shit-pit of a country.

And I started to panic.

The afternoon dragged on like a Bergman movie shown in slow-motion; not only was nothing happening, but it was happening at a snail's pace. The stress was almost unbearable. I kept peering out of the window, but there was no one to be seen. At one point I just wanted to have done with it; I felt like rushing into the street and shouting, confessing everything. But thankfully, the tattered remnants of self-preservation that I had somehow managed to hang on to, despite everything, prevented me from doing anything drastic. Instead, I just continued pacing up and down, a walking cliché; The Man with No Name, The Man with a Big Secret . . . the Man on the Run.

At about six o'clock, as dusk turned to darkness, I took swiftly to the streets, made my way via back alleys and side roads to the bus station, keeping out of the glare of the streetlamps and shop fronts, and purchased a ticket for a bus departing first thing the following morning.

Where was I going? I wasn't sure. All I knew was that I was heading south; as far south as you could go without crossing a border.

14

'Oh for Godsake William, don't start whingeing at me. It's hardly my fault if you can't put two words together. You don't hear me complaining about work. All you do is sit on your arse all day and wait for me to come home so that you can moan. Well I'm getting sick of it. I don't ask for any thanks; the fact that I keep you from starving to death in some garret does not, I feel, give me the right to insist on your gratitude. But I think it's damn thoughtless of you, when I've had a hard day at work, to greet me with a sour face and a whine. Now; where's my G and T?'

Yes folks, you guessed; that's the Big C talking.

It wasn't long before the feelings of inadequacy started to take hold. One of the major contributing factors was that I had all but abandoned hope of writing anything of any value. I suppose it goes without saying that this is a truly desperate state for a writer. However, if you're not a writer, then the full extent of that desperation cannot be known, cannot be comprehended.

For several years I had dedicated myself to the art, techniques and processes of creating fiction. In order to accomplish this with the seriousness required for such an endeavour, I had made a number of important sacrifices, not the least of which was being prepared to 'do without' in order to do the only thing that made any sense to me. No one was asking me to write, or indeed forcing me to; I was doing it out of choice, because it was what I wanted to do. But that didn't necessarily make it easy.

There is no denying that writing is a lonely occupation. It can also be – for the unpublished writer anyway – one of the least rewarding vocations one could pursue. And I don't just mean money. Before I started, I knew that the only way I could deal with the various pressures that would come with this way of life was to treat the entire exercise as if it were a real job, a proper 'nine-to-five' sort of job . . . without the monthly paycheque. What I did not realise was that the greatest problems would have nothing to do with a lack of financial remuneration, but with other, less tangible matters.

When you sit at a typewriter, all alone, grappling with nothing but words and concepts, there's no one to encourage you, to pat you on the back; no one to tell you what a good job you're doing. No one, in fact, to notice that you're doing anything at all. You receive none of the benefits of a regular job; you don't get to meet new people, you don't get to go to the pub with your workmates, you don't get to haggle for pay rises. There are no opportunities for promotion, no paid holidays, and no chance of nicking office stationery.

These may all seem small, petty matters, but put them together with the fact that there's no guaranteed cheque or wage packet at the end of the week, that in fact you may never see so much as a single cent for all your hard work, and it all adds up to a less than attractive package. Consequently, if you don't get any pleasure from the process, any joy from completing a sentence, a page, a chapter, then there really aren't any rewards at all. And if you're trying desperately to create something of merit, and it isn't working, then it can be an intensely depressing experience.

And if nothing at all is happening – no thoughts, no ideas, nothing – then it can be truly wretched. After all, what are you doing it for? The whole experience becomes pointless and, by extension, so do you. If you've dedicated your life to writing a novel, and there *is* no novel, then you just feel worthless and, at times, suicidal.

This is not a good starting point. Feeling worthless and suicidal is, by even the most cynical person's standards, a bad state to be in. However, if you have someone who loves you, someone who cares about you, who can soothe away some of the heartache at the end of a long day, banish those blues, inspire you with pep talks, build wilting confidence with a few choice compliments then maybe, just maybe, some of the strain can be alleviated. If you have someone who can make you look at yourself and laugh, then perhaps that can lighten your spirits.

But if you have someone who comes home at the end of the day and tells you that you're a waste of space, what do you do then? If you've had your teeth and claws removed so that you can no longer fight back, what happens next?

What happens, in particular, if you start looking inwards?

I'll tell you what happens; you find yourself in Big Trouble, that's what.

There was no novel, nor was there the likelihood of a

novel appearing, phantom-like yet fully formed, from out of the ether. In order to avoid adding guilt (guilt at not writing as opposed to all the other varieties with which I was already beset) to the growing number of debilitating factors that were already distressing my emotional health, I sought a compromise by sending some old short stories to various literary magazines. It was unlikely that they would be published, but at least the act of photocopying them and bundling them with a covering letter and stamped addressed envelope prior to despatch made me feel like I was doing something positive.

In the meantime, there were some home truths to face up to, not the least of which was the growing body of evidence suggesting that, when one got down to brass tacks, there really wasn't much I could give Cassandra. She didn't enjoy talking to me; we rarely had interesting conversations – no discussions on current affairs, no philosophical arguments on the state of the nation, no dialectical exchanges concerning the existence or otherwise of God. No, all our chit-chat was on a far more prosaic level; pass the fucking salt, get out of the frigging way, where are my sodding glasses . . . that sort of thing. We didn't share those gentle, loving moments that couples are so fond of, neither did we pleasure each other with little surprises: gifts, love notes, flowers. Even sex started to become routine. What started as an equitable working arrangement had become a market trade-off; bed and board for, I fear, bed and bored.

And I was the guilty party. At least, that was how I felt. Nothing I did seemed right. At first I put this down to a sense of simply feeling 'not good enough', that somehow I was quantitatively inadequate. It was only on reflection that I realised that it was not the calibre of my activities and abilities that were at fault, but the nature of them. When it came to impressing Cassandra, the category of functions that I now executed with such verve and dash could not, by definition, be expected to elicit anything more than a nod of recognition. No matter how beautifully I cleaned the floor, it would have been unreasonable to expect praise or admiration for my efforts: it's a clean floor – whoopee. My culinary exploits, regardless of quality, regardless of the amount of effort, time and tender loving care that was lavished on their preparation were – and could be nothing other than – meals; that is, something that is eaten now and unloaded later. Big deal. It really doesn't matter how expensive, aesthetically pleasing or delicious a meal is, it always ends up being flushed away. With this knowledge in mind, it is perhaps unreasonable to expect anyone to consider cooking (at any level other than professional) a noble occupation.

But I did. I did expect to be praised, petted and reassured, to be told that I was valuable, needed, wanted.

But it was not to be. Since moving in with Cassandra, my purpose in life had become primarily one of usefulness; I was a domestic and consequently I was awarded the same status as the washing machine or the vacuum cleaner. Except that Cassandra was right; I was not even as good as a machine. Machines don't whine, they don't sulk and they don't make excuses when, on using them for the third successive time in an evening, they fail.

Or – as happened on one particularly distressing occasion – break down completely.

My pride faltered. I watched my dignity evaporate. I sank slowly into a miasma of abasement and self-loathing, willing myself into submission like some masochistic flagellant. I was useless, hopeless and worthless and, what's more, it was all my fault. If Cassandra was critical then it was because she had the right to be critical. I didn't deserve her. I didn't deserve the comfort and freedom I had been given, the food, drink, board and lodging, wild sex and even, yes even pocket money: *I was not deserving*.

Shocked? Don't be. I should explain that all these feelings did not descend upon me suddenly, one morning say, whilst I was cleaning the oven. Oh no, it was much less dramatic than that. The process was gradual and insidious. At the start I was not even aware that there was anything wrong . . . not *really* wrong. A few concerns, yes. Some slight qualms perhaps. A nagging doubt here or there. But nothing that I could actually label or pinpoint, nothing that I could hold in the hand and say 'Wait; this stinks'. Besides, we are all prone to uncertainty in new situations.

However, by the time a further three months had passed, the amalgamation of Cassandra's attitudes towards me and my new-found knowledge concerning the evil disposition of men had given me a measure of my own unworthiness. By the time six months had passed, egged on by further reading and with no let-up from the Big C, my self-disgust had become so advanced that I could not understand why Cassandra was tolerating me.

By then I was in the firm grip of what I can only describe as a new and hitherto unknown virus that I labelled CAS: Continual Apology Syndrome. I was sorry. I was sorry, in fact, for everything. For not being happy, for not being glad, for being ungrateful, for not being rich, for listening too little, for talking too much, for forgetting a date, for remembering too late. I apologised for sleeping too much, working too little, complaining too often, looking too thin, sounding pathetic, being too noisy, asking too often, crying out loud, for being outrageous, walking too slowly, snoring too loudly, for being a man.

I was sorry I existed. And I apologised for that too. Profusely.

Not that this helped in any way. I suppose I should have known better, but by this stage I wasn't sure *what* I knew any more. I was, to say the least, a trifle confused, and what I had forgotten, in amongst all this worrying and fretting about doing the right thing, was that if there was one thing that Cassandra abhorred in another person, it was weakness. Cassandra was like a wild beast when it came to another's vulnerability, and would pounce instinctively upon lesser prey. Even if someone's deficiencies were not immediately apparent she liked nothing more than to sniff out their Achilles Heel and then sink her teeth in with relish. My cowering and snivelling became a self-destructive taunt, a red rag to a bull. In attempting to justify my existence I would fall back on recently discovered (and previously untapped) reserves of sycophancy, grovelling and shame and, of course, this only made matters worse.

I wallowed in this pathetic state for some considerable time, unable to see an escape or discover a way of vindicating myself in Cassandra's eyes. How could I raise my status and become more important to her with my self-belief in such tatters? Especially when her opinion had started off at such a low ebb. You may recall that Cassandra and I had built our liaison upon a foundation of mutual disgust. Whilst my opinion of Cassandra had changed dramatically, it was clear that she had not altered her feelings towards me one iota, and my adoption of a course of self-condemnation merely accorded well with Cassandra's viewpoint, strengthening her position in the relationship.

And oddly, the more self-demeaning and obsequious I became, the more Cassandra shone like a star. Inevitable really, as all I was actually doing was measuring the increasing distance between our stations. The further I sank into the mire of self-abomination and repugnance, the more glorious and godlike she became. I even took to telling her as much, only to be rebuked in language that, even by Cassandra's standards, was both shocking and curiously inventive. Did she not want me to tell her how beautiful she was, how unique? Despite her protestations, I still had enough of a grasp on the human condition to know that we all enjoy a little adulation now and then, even if we know how marvellous we are.

But it soon became evident that such an arrangement could not carry on indefinitely. It is difficult for you, I'm sure, to appreciate the strange depths of self-loathing to which I plummeted. It is all too easy to dismiss my confession as the rantings of a madman, but I assure you, I was not insane, and in relating the details of my descent, I swear that I have not exaggerated. This was no small matter, no minor identity crisis or loss of nerve. I knew things had hit an all-time low when I awoke one morning, looked into the bathroom mirror and threw up all over the sink. When you reach that stage, let me tell you, you have a serious problem. That was the morning I resolved to do something about it.

And, as if in answer to some mumbled prayer, the solution to my difficulties was handed to me on a silver platter. Or should I say, in a bedroom dresser?

I woke at dawn, brushed my teeth, threw on some

clothes and sat on the patio with a cup of coffee, watching the sky perform its chameleon act, metamorphosing from dark, opaque blues to brighter, more encouraging scarlet and pink hues, which echoed strongly inside me, a portent, hopefully, of things to come.

A note to the landlord on the kitchen table explained only that I had decided to move on. I had paid until the end of the week, so I knew there would be no comeback. I grabbed my shoulder bag with its meagre contents and, opening the door just a fraction to check if all was clear, quietly slipped away.

I walked cautiously to the bus station, following the same route that I had taken the previous evening. The city was just beginning to stir, and along the streets I saw a few natives – mostly street traders and destitutes – rising to begin the day. I was certain that no one was following me.

I boarded the rickety tin can that masqueraded as a bus and sat on the back seat, examining my fellow passengers as they boarded in turn. There were no other foreigners as far as I could tell; they were all locals, mostly men, and they paid me scant attention. Once the bus was filled to capacity, the driver started the engine and, with a great (though probably misplaced) sense of relief, we were soon trundling down the main drag that led out of the city. A few shops and stalls were readying themselves for business as the dilapidated vehicle wheezed and lumbered down the road, like an old man with asthma.

The sun, a flaming amber balloon, had already lifted above the horizon, ready to cast its strangely cool illumination onto the surrounding landscape, throwing everything into sharp relief and casting sinister shadows across the ground. A dark-skinned child with ebony eyes and ragged clothes harried his mother while she built a small fire by the roadside to boil a pot of water, whilst another child – naked save for a ripped and grubby t-shirt – poked about in the dust with a splintered piece of wood.

The shops and buildings gradually thinned out and before long we were on dirt tracks that snaked through a barren world of dust and rocks. The bus picked up speed as it headed into the desert, careening around bends and swaying dangerously across the width of the road, the driver seemingly oblivious to the oncoming traffic, which was composed mostly of trucks and the occasional ox-drawn cart. The bus shook and bounced alarmingly as the driver sought out every single pit and pot-hole. Each jerk and jolt jarred my spine, sending a short, sharp shock-wave up through my back. I braced my knees against the seat in front to avoid being hurled around each time the bus took a corner too fast, but this technique was of little use and by the time an hour had passed my knees were bruised and tender. I resigned myself to ten hours of extreme discomfort and allowed the dreary, empty landscape beyond the cracked, grimy windows to lull me into a trance and hypnotise me into submission.

The desert was another great disappointment; this was no Sahara with huge, windswept, sinusoidal dunes marching into the distance. This was scrub-desert, a dry, uninviting monotony of sand and rock, punctuated here and there by the occasional sickly tree rising gnarled and deformed from some piss-hole wadi or dried-out stream, like the withered arm of a drowning man. And this desperate, inhospitable landscape stretched as far as one could see, without relief: a waste land.

The bus stopped two or three times during the journey at small, dilapidated villages where sad, wizened old men served sweet tea in chipped clay cups to the comatosed passengers, and offered oily, unappetising snacks to the hungry. In all these villages the stench of death and decay lingered in the atmosphere, as if the only thing that the inhabitants had to look forward to was the final release from the toil and hardship that circumscribed their pathetic lives.

The view from the bus only compounded my growing unease. I didn't know what lay ahead, what would greet me at the end of the road, and this lack of knowledge combined with the evident lack of preparation made me doubt the wisdom of this latest move. What was I doing here, thousands of miles from civilisation, from home, from everything I knew? What on earth did I think I was doing?

Then I remembered.

I was running away.

I was relieved when the light began to fail so that I wouldn't have to gaze out onto all this misery and desolation.

I arrived at my destination sore, tired, and extremely depressed.

15

We are none of us truly wise. We're all just children, playing at life as if it were a game. And like kids, we enter into the whole pretence with a naïve amalgamation of awe and confusion. The world is our playground, but we don't know the rules, so we stumble along blindly in the hope that we will, somehow, prevail and – if lucky – win the game. The prize? That most elusive of treasures; pleasure.

The trouble is, of course, that none of us really know what pleasure is. Someone – I forget who – defined pleasure as that which we feel when experience exceeds expectation, which is all well and good, but frankly, it doesn't give much hope to those of us with high expectations or even half-way decent imaginations. Whatever its nature, when pleasure arrives, origin unknown, one thing is guaranteed; for a moment, maybe as fleeting as the time it takes to complete a belly laugh or lose consciousness in the tremors of orgasm . . . for that one moment we are fooled into believing that the world is good and that life is fair. It is the most potent illusion of all.

So we search for it, seek it out, even hunt it down as if it were a wild beast. Our transatlantic cousins even enshrine the hunt in their Declaration of Independence, where the pursuit of happiness is guaranteed as a basic human right.

The key to pleasure, of course, is wisdom. Wisdom banishes confusion. Wisdom allows us to be selective. Wisdom will show us what is, and what is not, pleasurable. Through wisdom, we believe we will find the answers; through wisdom we will find an endless supply of pleasure. So we turn to the wise and ask them to help us, to tell us the rules so we can play the game better, so we can win, so we can get more pleasure.

And here lies the greatest paradox of all, because if we were wise, we would know that, like the pot of gold at rainbow's end, the fount of wisdom is a myth; a myth perpetrated by the scared to satisfy the insecure. If we were wise, we would make wise decisions. We would not eat junk food, we would not smoke tobacco, we would not have unprotected sex in an era when such things may be fatal. We would not pollute our rivers nor irradiate the atmosphere. We would not murder defenceless men, women and children and dignify the act with a label, war, which by its very existence some-how suggests a justification for such terrible deeds. If we were wise we would feed, clothe and house the people of the world rather than squander our resources on weapons of mass destruction. If we were wise, we would not seek pleasure, we would not hunt it like an escaped convict or killer shark.

And if we were truly wise, we would not teach that there exists a kind and merciful God who – quite sensibly, given His evident failure – never shows His face. If women were wise they would tell men what they were doing wrong. If men were wise, they would listen.

* * *

167

Let us return, for a moment, to a house in Hampstead, to a bathroom, a worried man and a sink full of vomit. It is not a pretty picture, I grant you, but it is important to examine the situation carefully in order to clarify an otherwise confused scenario.

The head of the house (the breadwinner, the one who calls the shots, the one who wears the trousers . . . the one with the real balls) is out. The dutiful sub-dominant partner, the one who does the housework and the cooking, has just struck bottom. He has peered into the mirror, in much the same way as he has done every day for most of his life, only on this occasion, seeing his own reflection has provoked a disgust so advanced that it has, in turn, elicited a second – and quite involuntary – look at his breakfast.

In his deeply confused and rather unsteady state, he has just sufficient presence of mind to recall, albeit vaguely, that six months previously he was a reasonably well-balanced individual struggling to break into the hallowed halls of authorship. He remembers that friends and acquaintances once thought him intelligent and wilful, an amusing companion with a witty collection of pithy one-liners and an amusing line in self-deprecative remarks. People usually enjoyed his company, and no one had ever been sufficiently angered or upset by him to hit, slap or strike him at any time. Overall, if we wanted to sum up briefly, we would probably refer to him as 'a good sort', a man possessed of few pretensions who, whilst not suffering fools gladly, would never insult one to his or her face.

As he turns on the hot tap to clean the sink, it occurs to him that he has come a long way in six months, and most of the journey – eventful though it may have seemed – has been resolutely downhill. Unfortunately, he has been conditioned so effectively and emasculated with such single-minded precision, that he is only able to see in two-dimensions; that is, he is unable to step outside of his predicament and view it from a different perspective. Consequently, even though he realises that something is amiss (even *he* senses that throwing up at the sight of your own reflection is cause for concern) he concludes that the only way to effect a solution is to tackle the problem from within.

This is his first mistake.

I crept into Cassandra's empty room. If anyone could have seen me they would have initiated a citizen's arrest solely on the grounds that I appeared so suspicious that it was evident I was about to commit, at the very least, a misdemeanour. But was I? It is true that I was about to step over some sort of boundary, and that I was doing this with full knowledge and that some might see this as a crime. But if my actions were criminal, then as I tiptoed across the carpet towards the dressing table, I had not yet established either motive or goal.

I crouched down in front of the dressing table and tugged at the bottom drawer. As expected, it was locked. As far as I knew there was no spare key, and even if there had been, I had no idea where Cassandra might keep it. I stared at the drawer for a few minutes wondering how to proceed; I could not let a simple matter of locks keep me from my objective. Unfortunately, of the many skills I had acquired through the years, lock-picking was not among them. Clearly some sort of lateral thinking was required. I had to find a way of getting into the drawer without Cassandra knowing. Forcing the lock was out of the question, as would be any attempt to dismantle the piece of furniture in question. No, it had to be something much simpler than that. Then something occurred to me.

There were three drawers in the base of the dresser, of which only the bottom one had a lock. The other two had no such security arrangements. I pulled the handles of the drawer above the locked one and, lo and behold, out it slid. Two small catches either side stopped the drawer from slipping off its runners, but with the aid of my ever-trusty Swiss army knife (a gift, I recalled at a later date, from a previous girlfriend – ah, the ever marvellous manifestations of irony) these catches were soon unclipped and the drawer came neatly away.

There, in the now exposed bottom drawer, nestling on a stack of silky underwear, none of which I had seen before, was a black ring-binder. It just rested there like a precious jewel, and as I lifted it gently from its hiding place, I half expected it to hum with a deep resonance or burst into flames like something out of an Indiana Jones movie. But it did no such thing. I weighed the folder thoughtfully in my hands, anxious to feel not just the weight of the object itself, but the gravity of the event. For, even in my haste and confusion, I was still aware that I had just walked straight into a real-life cliché: the point of no return.

How easily that moment passed; how innocent my smile, how ingenuous my intentions. I replaced the drawer and exited, exhibiting – nay, experiencing – neither feelings of guilt nor guile. I returned to the front room, sat upon the sofa, opened up the binder and examined the typescript that lay therein.

If, as I claimed then (and claimed later in my defence) I entered the room immaculate, devoid of premeditated motive, then alas I cannot profess that I was in the same

state of grace after I had read the contents of the mysterious folder.

The Fall of Man: an unashamedly feminist tract
by
Cassandra Beauchamp

Perhaps the title should have warned me. Throughout
my life there have been times when I've had to wonder if
I possess even the most basic powers of deduction. It
is not, I think, irrelevant that I spent so much of my
adolescence and young adulthood thirstily drinking in
the words of my elders without question. That I should
have assumed others' words were imbued, somehow,
with virtue is colourful testament to my naïvety. Which
is why – having seen the title and taken no notice of its
implications – I read on with curiosity, safe and secure in
my profound ignorance.

Why was I not taught, as a child perhaps, that evil
lurks at every corner? Why had I not assumed the seemingly natural defence mechanisms towards words that I
had towards flailing fists?

Rather than engaging caution, I started to examine
Cassandra's cauldron of noxious ingredients with innocent indulgence, drawing heavily on the poisonous
fumes as if they were no more harmful than the vapours
of attar of roses. This was my second mistake. By the
time I realised the truth about Cassandra's typescript,
it was too late. Like the inexperienced postulant who,
stranded in a bookshop to shelter from a storm, inno-
cently scans a book entitled *Naturism* in the belief he
will learn something about flora and fauna, I was both
shocked and amazed by what I saw, and yet was unable

171

– despite immediate misgivings – to abstain from further examination.

Actually, shocked is far too restrained a term to express how I felt. It is difficult now, even with the benefit of hindsight, to conjure the real sense of what I experienced in those first few moments, the torrid combination of nausea, revulsion and morbid fascination that pulsed through me, took hold of my guts with a steely grip, and drew the blood from my face. As with a gruesome horror film, I was both sickened and consumed by what I saw, compelled to view despite my reactions, despite my better judgement.

I read what amounted to just over one hundred double-spaced pages. It was very much a 'work-in-progress', but despite its innumerable corrections and typographical errors, it was a very readable and erudite piece of work. That Cassandra was capable of writing both eloquently and intelligently came as no surprise; I had always suspected that her sneering and belittling of 'aspiring writers' was nothing but bluff (or perhaps taunt), and that she secretly harboured a strong desire to put pen to paper. She was too well read, her manner too rhetorical for her to have anything but a deep, perhaps even passionate respect for words. No, what was so shocking – and ultimately distressing – was her subject matter.

It was all about me.

And having absorbed the typescript in its entirety, and feeling both bewildered and exhausted, I knew that I could not ignore it. On the contrary; in that fleeting, irreversible moment, I sensed that I had discovered my salvation and that, consequently, I must act to make best use of it.

And that, my friends, was mistake number three.

16

I stared at the three envelopes lying face down on the hallway carpet. I had reached a stage in my writing career where I knew instinctively when the mail was for me. I could also tell without closer examination if said letters were addressed by my own fair hand. Sixth-sense? Precognition perhaps? Who knows. Whatever it was, it was a thoroughly useless talent.

The fledgling writer becomes inured to the rejection slip; I had read that somewhere. However, having been reared in the 'don't believe everything you read' school of scepticism, I would still rant and rave at the casual and occasionally caustic manner in which an editor had dismissed several weeks – perhaps months – of work with a curt: 'Sorry, not for us'.

Now then, answer me this; why isn't the rest of life as easy as that? Why can't we confront the Inland Revenue, say, with equal impunity? Here, Mister Taxman; please find enclosed the returned tax bill, unpaid and unwanted. I am afraid it does not meet my requirements at this time. Might I suggest you try elsewhere. Or: Dear Mother/Father/Wife/Husband/Friend/Lover; after much consideration, and having examined the evidence carefully, I am sorry to inform you that you do not fit my list. However, I'd like to take this opportunity of thanking you for your time and trouble, and wish you every success in the future.

Yes, let's have a change around here; let's all be editors. Here God, please find enclosed your copious doctrines, indecipherable dogmas, ludicrous precepts and wholly unacceptable laws. They are being returned; they have been rejected. The same goes for you, Government; I have read your proposals thoroughly and I'm afraid your ideas are unsound, repetitious and smack of terminological inexactitudes. I wish you luck placing them elsewhere.

Yes, let's all wield this extraordinary control; let's all hold the power of acceptance or rejection in our hands, and make life-changing decisions based on nothing more than personal preference or whim. Let's all have the power of awarding or withdrawing; let us all giveth and taketh away. Because the fact is, it's all completely arbitrary. Don't you see? The time has come to stop believing that other people know better than we do; the time has come for us to stop believing that anybody – whatever their profession, standing, intelligence – actually *knows* anything. It is time to face facts; none of us is wise.

That morning the mail told a familiar enough story. A well known satirical magazine had rejected a short story on the grounds that it wasn't funny (a response which, ironically, I thought hilarious). A major literary monthly thought another story 'atmospheric' (which I presumed was a euphemism for 'lightweight but otherwise devoid of literary merit'), whilst someone a TV company 'could not go with the narrative drive' of my submission, which could have meant almost anything, although I suspect it was just longhand for 'worthless piece of crap'. Ah well, as someone once said, these things are sent to try us, which no doubt translates somewhere along the line as 'give up while you're still ahead'.

Having read these rejections I allowed myself my usual five minutes of cursing and breast-beating, and then settled down to the daily round of duties. But for some reason (please don't laugh), my heart wasn't in the ironing that morning. Something was bothering me.

A few minutes later I found myself walking nervously along the High Street with Cassandra's typescript clamped tightly under my arm. I must have looked guilty as hell, as if I was carrying a consignment of illegal drugs or a folder full of hard pornography. I felt sure that everyone was looking at me. I even saw one couple, chatting amiably enough on a street corner, stop their conversation and point towards me. It was almost enough to make me rush back to the house and forget the whole thing. But somehow I kept my nerve, and ten minutes later, the deed was done.

It cost ten pounds to have the entire script photo-copied, which is a lot of money for someone struggling without a personal income and making do on hand-outs. But I viewed it as an investment. Somehow I knew that, one way or another, my impetuous speculation would pay off.

Having returned the original to its rightful place, I took off once again to a nearby café with the copy to examine it more closely. Although in all the time I had lived with Cassandra she had never once arrived home from work before six in the evening, I didn't dare take any risks; I didn't want to think what might happen to me if she caught me in the act of reading her secret papers.

I spent the rest of the morning studying the first few pages in detail. As you have no doubt experienced for yourself, it is one thing to hear or read something of a shocking or controversial nature for the very first time when, innocent and without expectation, you are taken unawares. It is a quite different experience to re-examine it in the unemotional and unambiguous 'cold light of day'.

In this instance, although the contents of the document remained no less surprising, they were somehow less devastating. This is not a contradiction in terms; my first reaction on reading Cassandra's manuscript had been sheer, unadulterated horror; it was as if the world beneath my feet had lost all pretence of substance. In the café that morning I was able to review the contents from a slightly more distanced perspective and assess the material with a more analytical eye. It was still an upsetting experience, but at least I could keep it in proportion.

I was not yet sure of my reasons for reading the manuscript a second time, nor was I clear about what I might gain from it; all I knew was that I had to understand as clearly as possible what had really been happening between Cassandra and me, and how these pages not only reflected upon the relationship, but how they would influence it from here on. I also had a sense that, somehow, they would provide an answer to my predicament. Whatever, as confused as I was, I started to take notes. And to give you some idea of the nature of Cassandra's work, read, if you will, part of the preface.

The Fall of Man is based upon the results of a unique study in interpersonal relationships, the first of its kind to be undertaken in contemporary Western society. In this study – which drew its inspiration and genesis from Feminist Ideology whilst employing the methodology and practical applications of Experimental Psychology –

a male subject was enlisted to undergo a complete reversal of the social, psychological and gender roles normally associated with men in this part of the late twentieth century. The subject was – over a period of a year, and without his knowing – to be deliberately and insidiously coerced into assuming a role frequently associated with women; that of the dependent housewife, with all the moral, physical and psychological disadvantages that accompany the position, and to study his reactions and responses.

For the purposes of this study it was imperative that the subject be of above average intelligence, seemingly wilful and yet at all times unaware that the process he was enduring was both deliberate and meaningful. To instigate a study of the 'hen-pecked husband' was to be avoided at all costs, as this phenomenon, whilst widespread, is still something of an anomaly and tends to be based on very specific (rather than universal) circumstances. Consequently it was necessary to search out a man who was both self-employed and financially insecure, yet not completely impoverished (this was *not* an investigation of contemporary slavery). It was important that he would be adjudged able to adapt to the 'tasks' of the housewife, which necessitated having sufficient time and energy to carry out the day-to-day chores. He would have to be, initially, financially dependent upon the woman of the house. One aim of the study was to see if, in time, he would also become both emotionally and intellectually subservient.

The rewards of my own career had endowed me with many of the necessary requirements to take on the role of Partner in this research. I own a large, comfortable home ideally suited for the purpose of the experiment. Additionally, my university training in applied and social psychology had equipped me with suitable skills to play 'the female breadwinner' and, of course, monitor and analyse the proceedings.

I took it upon myself to search out a suitable guinea pig, a task in itself of some considerable complexity (for further details see Appendix 1.1). After three months the ideal subject was discovered at a private party held, for the record, by a mutual acquaintance, and throughout this document he will be referred to as William. William was an unpublished, aspiring novelist of limited talent who had, prior to the start of the experimental period, abandoned regular, paid employment in order to become a freelance writer. At the time of our meeting he was, therefore, officially self-employed but with no steady income to speak of, and was subsisting on a meagre weekly allowance culled from his own savings and incidental freelance work. He was thus an ideal candidate for the study.

I should add at this point that the unusual nature of the territory which was being explored necessitated certain personal interactions of a highly sexual nature, many of which are described in precise detail (See: Ch. 4, 5, 8 and 9). Some readers of a more sensitive disposition may find the graphic nature of the descriptions and the language in these encounters upsetting. It is important to note that, in all instances, these encounters were considered essential to the success of the experiment. Participating in these interactions was perhaps the most formidable and uncomfortable aspect of the entire study; remaining emotionally detached whilst not alerting the subject proved particularly difficult. Consequently, I wish it to be a matter of record that, despite the seemingly intimate nature of the physical relations, I remained, to all intents and purposes, 'emotionally virgin'. It is, I realise, a fine distinction, but I make a point of this not as a disclaimer to slave a troubled conscience, but merely in order that the reader does not misinterpret any of the actions taken during the course of the study. At all times I approached the experiment in the serious, scholarly manner required for a study of this kind. As a human being and a woman it was vital that I maintain a barrier of impersonal indifference lest I be swayed or distracted from the task in hand, or, worse still, become trapped emotionally in the relationship, thus rendering the results null and void.

Now do you see?

No, you don't. I know what you're thinking: revenge. 'He's going to get his own back. She's made a complete fool of him and now he's on the warpath . . .'

Is this what you think? If so, how little you understand me. True enough, she had made a complete fool of me; worse still, I had – in her very own words – been nothing more than a guinea pig. But, I confess, other than being sorely offended by her remark that I was an 'aspiring novelist of limited talent', I was more intrigued than vengeful. I expect this was because I was in a state of shock.

Of course, this isn't to say I wasn't also very upset. Of course I was; in a word, I was shattered. But I was not vengeful. You see, there is one thing that you may have forgotten. By now I was in love with Cassandra. I was besotted, head over heels, entranced. I could no more deliberately harm her than I could fly of my own volition; I was incapable of revenge. Even if I had been just a pawn in her game, a rat in her maze, I was still mad about Cassandra. And I only had to think for a moment about the things she had done for me, about my dirty dreams come true, to know that, despite what I had just read, despite the evidence of my own eyes, there was no way that she could be anything other than deeply attached to me. I mean, a woman just couldn't do those things for a man unless she loved him, could she? Well, could she?

Oh God; see what I mean about my understanding of women? Pathetic, isn't it. Of course, any normal man would probably have packed up and scarpered ages ago. Think what you will about Cassandra's assertions of remaining 'emotionally virgin' (and how this tallies with allowing a man about whom you feel nothing to sodomise you on a regular basis for six months). The fact that I had remained in this 'relationship' until this stage, allowing myself to be put upon and manipulated in so

179

brutal and cold-blooded a fashion, reflects a good deal more on me than it does on Cassandra. After all, she was just doing what all good research students do (ha bloody ha). I know this now, of course, and see what a fool I was to allow myself to be coerced and influenced so strongly, but at the time . . . well, remember, we're dealing with a man whose self-esteem is so low that he throws up when he looks in the mirror. I think that probably tells you more about my state of mind than anything.

No, I did not run away and no, I did not sit up half the night plotting ways to exact my revenge. On the contrary, reading Cassandra's manuscript for the second time only convinced me more than ever that I had to prove myself to her, that I had to change myself from a rat in a maze to the man of her dreams, from her experiment in feminist politics to the very love of her life . . .

What was this? Was I mad? Undoubtedly. In love? Indubitably. Beyond help? Alas, without a shadow of a doubt. It was too late for me. I had become incapable of thinking like a sane, rational *man*. In fact, that was part of my difficulty. After everything I had read in Cassandra's dangerous little collection, I no longer *wanted* to be logical and rational like men. Men were terrible beings; look at all the dreadful things they did. Look at how they behaved towards other men, the animal kingdom, the planet. Look at how they treated women. No, I wanted to be sympathetic, emotional, instinctive; I wanted to be all the things that women said men weren't; all the things, I thought, that women wanted.

It just gets worse, doesn't it? It's pitiable. In the same way that a horse can be led but may not drink, so it is with men and feminism. Monkey see, monkey do, but monkey still not have a fucking clue. I had drunk of the fountain of wisdom, but it had not made me wise. I had clutched hold of the wrong end of the stick with such fervour and determination that it had become fused to my grubby little hand, and now all I could do was beat myself about the head with it.

This was my plan: I would prove to Cassandra that I was not chauvinist, ignorant, thoughtless, cruel, 'typically' male. The reading I had done of the books on Cassandra's lowest shelf would stand me in good stead. I was now *au fait* with all the arguments, concurred with the accusations, agreed with the conclusions. My stance, henceforth, would be unequivocal; feminism was the most important intellectual and political movement of the late twentieth century. I would declare my allegiance, I would renounce sexism, I would be a convert for the cause. Thus armed I would prove to her that I was a New Man; considerate, fair, empathetic, free of the old social conditioning and unfettered by conventions of sex-differences. I would come out in favour of women's rights and equal opportunities. I would denounce patriarchy for the insidious and ruinous doctrine that it was. I would espouse with great sensitivity my newly acquired beliefs, confessing that personal experience had provided the revelation. That, in fact, it was all down to Cassandra, that she had been my saviour. Having adopted the role of housewife I now had real insight into the predicament of women the world over. I would prove to Cassandra that her experiment had been a success, and that my new position had made me see the light. I would prove to her that, without question, I had changed; that I was enlightened.

But, my friends, I was not enlightened. I was not even

moderately illuminated. My subsequent course of action proves that beyond doubt.

I was still Cassandra's Clown.

17

'You're pathetic.'

'I'm just trying to do the right thing.'

'Stop trying William; it's becoming tedious in the extreme.'

'Cassandra . . .'

'You're whining; I've told you before, I can't stand it when you whine. What is wrong with you? My God, it's all I ever hear these days. Sometimes I think you do it deliberately to annoy me. I didn't get into this relationship just to placate you day in day out.'

'Well if you don't mind me asking, what *did* you enter into this relationship for?'

'Oh dear, here we go again; the perennial self-doubt of the creative nobody . . .'

'I don't know what you want!'

'Don't shout at me William. I have a headache . . .'

What? No, go on, say it. Well you're wrong.

During the weeks that followed my discovery of *The Fall of Man*, it dawned on me that I might well have missed my vocation. Instead of struggling to be a writer, I could have busked it as an actor.

Forgive me my lack of humility, but really, you should

have seen me. The RSC could not have faulted my performance.

What do you mean, you don't see any difference? Of *course* not. That's the whole point. Now that I knew what was going on, I wasn't about to blow it. Cassandra wanted a fawning, emasculated weed; that, after all, was primarily what her grand experiment was all about. So that is what I gave her, in a performance that differed, externally, not one jot from my previous behaviour. To suddenly come over fearless, well balanced and wise, spouting feminist rhetoric like some lesbian propagandist would have ruined everything. If she twigged that I had seen the typescript and wised up, then it would all be over, and I'd probably have found myself back in my dismal Turnpike Lane bedsit faster than you could say 'you cunning, sexist bastard'. This way, I could 'role play' to my heart's content, knowing I was one step ahead of her all the time.

Better than that, I could even start to anticipate moves in advance. If, in reality, I was the star of the show, then there seemed to me no reason why I could not start writing my own lines. If previously I had been the unwitting creator of the studied scenarios, then armed with my new knowledge I could now be the wilful author of my destiny. You think this is just a theory? Think again. The results of my new-found knowledge, as you will see for yourself, had a dramatic and conspicuous effect upon *The Fall of Man*.

The day after I procured a copy of the typescript I tried a little experiment. That evening when Cassandra came home I greeted her, as usual, with a G and T and foot massage. Then I did something that I hoped would take her by surprise. I made a little confession.

'Cassandra.'

184

'Hmmm?'

'I don't want you to take this the wrong way but, well, I've been feeling a bit miserable lately . . .'

'Please William, not now; you know how I feel about this.'

'Yes, yes, I know . . . I'm not going to moan. I was just wondering if, after dinner, you'd take me out . . . a drink, a film maybe. We haven't been out in ages – not that I'm complaining – and I just thought it would be nice to do something together for a change. If you're really too tired, I'll understand, only . . . well, it's hard being cooped up in the house all day, and I'd be ever so grateful . . .'

Okay, so maybe it was a touch obvious, but let me tell you; it did the trick. The glimmer of a smile creased her lips as she sipped from her glass. I have never claimed clairvoyant powers before, but I swear at that moment I could read her mind: You're learning at last.

She agreed. She tucked into the chicken casserole I had prepared with relish and, after I had done the dishes, she took me to see the new Meryl Streep film at The Screen on the Hill, which was very good. She even bought me popcorn. I enjoyed the evening immensely; and I let her know about it.

A week later I searched out the ever-growing type-script and examined the new pages. And in amongst them, this is what I found:

As predicted, about half-way through the study, William, who was by now well-entrenched in his new circumstances, began to develop and execute certain skills that had hitherto been absent. These skills – commonly referred to as 'feminine wiles' sat uneasily with the subject, but none the less he was prepared to use them in order to satisfy certain needs. Instead of whimpering and complaining, he began requesting special attention, careful at all times not to aggravate me or make it appear he was being demanding. I chose to respond favourably, and his gratitude was truly remarkable. It was clear that he had learned an important principle, either consciously or otherwise; that I had indulged him, and that he was privileged. This was a turning point in the transformation, and showed that at long last he was beginning to accept his role and live with it, and even explore its possibilities, rather than fight it continually, only to lose out at every turn.

Scorer, if you please, chalk one up for Bill Smith.

Now don't get me wrong; this was not a competition; I had no wish to outsmart Cassandra. A Pyrrhic victory (easily attained now that I was on to her) was of no use to me. What good to win the battle and lose the war? If Cassandra knew that I was clued up, I would be out on my ear in no time. No, what was important here was that I was able to re-establish my identity for myself and as a result, rather than fall continually into the traps that Cassandra was setting, I could lower myself into them gently, and then crawl out again when she wasn't looking. As long as I understood what was happening, I had no reason to be afraid. And in the meantime I could begin, slowly but surely, to win her over.

And I knew how I would do it, too.

Moving south was the most sensible decision I've taken since arriving in this wretched country. I could have done without the spine-shattering bus ride, mind, but there is – as I've learned many times – a price to pay for everything.

I arrived at the end of the line – a seedy resort town on the coast – at dusk, an otherwise romantic time in most Mediterranean and Levantine countries. Although, as far as I was concerned, all it meant was that I had about half an hour to find some place to stay before darkness swamped the area, not a pleasant prospect for a coward such as I.

Thankfully, a small notice pinned near the indecipherable timetable advertised a traveller's hostel nearby. The note was in English and French and, having copied down the diagram that mapped the route from the bus station, I headed off to find a bed for the night. Thankfully I found it with relative ease. As it was situated just five minutes walk from the bus station I considered it a personal triumph that I was able to locate it in just under twenty minutes.

Luck, however, was not exactly cheering me on from the stands as, by the time I arrived, the place was fully booked. The manager, a splendidly amicable though curiously misplaced Welshman, apologised for the lack of beds but assured me that if I cared to kip on the sofa in the common room, he could promise me a bona fide resting place for the following night. As I had no desire to go traipsing around a completely unfamiliar town in the pitch dark, I accepted his offer. Although at some time during the previous few days I had taken on the demeanour of a dispossessed immigrant, I tried as best I could to make myself familiar with my new environment.

'The Resthouse', the notice at the station had assured me, had a reputation for 'cordiality and informality', an atmosphere that presumably encouraged intimacy and friendly social intercourse. However, having dumped my gear in the corner of the common room, my immediate assessment of my fellow guests was that they were possessed by what amounted to nothing more than blithe indifference.

Was I bothered? Surely not; after all, hadn't I deliberately been seeking solitude so as not to be interfered with? Wasn't the prospect of a bunch of similarly displaced yet overly familiar Europeans, anxious to strike up acquaintance, just about the last thing I wanted? You'd have thought so. But in truth, at that moment, it was not the case. It had been several days since I had left England, and in all that time I had probably spoken no more than two dozen words, and most of those had been expressly to demand information. The fact was, I was desperate to talk to someone. Not anyone, not just some man in the street; I needed a friendly face, an understanding manner; I needed, more than anything, a confessor – the sort that listens as opposed to the ones that spout. I needed someone to hear my sins.

Perhaps under different circumstances I might have just taken to the floor and yelled 'Hello folks, I'm here!' but of course I was in no position to draw that sort of attention to myself. Besides, the expressions of those assembled in the common room, their eyes glued to the video currently exploding in a riot of noise and colour on the television, suggested I would achieve nothing by such a provocative gambit, save perhaps a few expressions of annoyance for having interrupted their evening's entertainment.

Instead I found an empty patch of floor space and settled down uncomfortably to gaze, with little interest, at the fictional events taking place on the screen. A large oriental gentleman was, at that precise moment, kicking the shit out of an even larger and certainly uglier foe, neither of whom had evidently had much truck with the Stanislavsky method. Or, indeed, acting tuition of any kind. This was garbage of the sort that, even in my most depraved soap-opera junkie days, I would not have

188

deemed worthy of attention. My fellow viewers however were so entranced by the action that I concluded, there and then, that I had made yet another stupendous error, and was about to spend the first of several nights in an institute for the terminally deranged.

However, unbeknown to me, salvation was at hand, albeit in a most unlikely guise.

'This would have to rate as the worst movie I've ever seen,' said a broadly transatlantic voice from over my right shoulder. Now, under normal circumstances, this would have had me shuffling to my feet and making for the nearest exit with all due haste. It isn't that I *dislike* Americans . . . well, actually, yes it is. Not all Americans of course; just the noisy ones. (And, incidentally, in case you've ever wondered why it is that American tourists *are* so loud, the answer is simple: it's so that they can be heard above their clothes.)

Consequently, it was with trembling hands and heavy heart that I turned, looked up, and came face to face with a curly-haired, clean shaven and rather pleasant looking young man whose warm smile and sparkling eyes gave – unlikely as it may seem – an impression of sympathetic intelligence.

'Are all the movies they show as bad as this?' I said, nodding towards the box.

'I've no idea; I only arrived today.' He shook his head in a parody of disbelief, then thrust his hand forward. 'David Kessler,' he said, rather formally, I thought, for an American.

'Bill Smith,' I replied too swiftly. The words had tumbled out of my mouth with such eagerness that it was only as the sounds hit the air that I realised what I had done. Since arriving in the country I had told no one my real name. It wasn't that I truly hoped to remain

189

incognito – after all, the officers at passport control had examined my passport at Immigration on arrival. But I just felt safer walking around knowing that no one here knew who I was. But now I had spoken it out loud.

'Good to meet you Bill,' said my new confidant. His grip was solid and restrained, a far cry from the bone-crushing and energetic experience I had come to expect from young American males hoping to make an immediate and devastating impression. 'I've just about had it with Kung Fu over there. Wanna go grab a beer somewhere?'

I cringed momentarily at the unfamiliar colloquialisms and wondered whether, bright eyes or not, this fellow would be capable of speaking about anything other than baseball and cars. Then I looked around me and figured that half an hour in his company could be no worse than the same period spent among the zombie screen-watchers.

'Sounds good to me,' I said, getting to my feet. 'I'll just get my jacket.'

David had arrived that afternoon and, showing the sort of pragmatic initiative that I clearly lacked, had discovered the location of three bars, all within walking distance. We headed to the nearest one, situated around the corner from 'Dai's Pit' (as it soon became known, not altogether affectionately) and sat at a rusting, rickety table encrusted with dog-ends and peanut shells, where we drank thirstily from chilled glasses.

'So whereabouts are you from?' I asked politely, praying that he would not state the obvious.

'Delaware; ever heard of it?'

'Uh-huh. I even passed through it once. Quickly.'

In truth, I had never been to Delaware, but I knew

from other sources that it was little more than an industrial wasteland, and not the sort of place one would visit out of choice. When David laughed, I thought it too much to hope that he had caught the implicitly derogatory nature of my false confession.

But I was wrong.

'I don't blame you in the least. Best thing about Delaware is the turnpike heading north. And you; you're English?'

'A Londoner . . .' and so on. It was like talking with a normal human being. The conversation remained light but sharp, and soon suggested to me that, where David was concerned, I might have cause to reconsider my deep-seated prejudices.

We spent the remainder of the evening in the bar, chatting amiably – smalltalk mostly – and as the evening wore on I realised how much I had missed this sort of thing. After all, I had not had a decent, reasonably intelligent conversation with another man for a very long time. I warmed to David and his easy manner and amusing stories, which managed to take my mind off my immediate problems. David listened eagerly, too, not wanting to hog the conversation. Towards the end of the evening, my tongue loosened a little by the beer, my guard lowered just a touch, I found myself wanting to tell him more, tell him about what had happened to me. I wanted to tell him everything, the whole story.

But I couldn't. At least, not directly.

The only uncomfortable note came as we were wandering back to the hostel. We were still chatting easily when, out of the blue, David asked me what I did for a living. It was an innocent enough question, but I hesitated; how much did I want David to know about me? Wasn't it bad enough that he knew my name? I

191

thought about it for a moment then figured I was being overly cautious; after all what difference could it make?

So I told him.

'You write? That's fantastic. Have I read your stuff?'

'I doubt it. I've had some things published . . . but it's no big deal.'

'No big deal! You crazy?' Even though it was late and we had been talking for what seemed like half the night, David suddenly became very animated. 'God, I've always wanted to write. It must be *so* fantastic. And published! You don't know what that sounds like to someone like me.'

'It's really not that great an accomplishment.' I suddenly felt a little embarrassed by David's enthusiasm, although I wasn't sure why. 'Anyone can write; it's just a matter of acquiring some basic techniques then applying yourself . . .'

'Bullshit,' said David. He narrowed his eyes and shook his head. 'You write fiction?'

'Sure. Some.'

'Well, that's not just technique and application. You have to have talents, abilities . . . you have to have an imagination.'

'And you haven't?'

'Sure, but it doesn't work that way. Believe me, I've tried. I've spent most of my adult life trying to write a novel. But it's not in me. I'm basically too honest.'

'Too honest?'

'Yeah. Writing fiction is just a controlled form of lying. You make it all up, right?'

'Well yes but . . .'

'You take the truth and you twist it. You distort realities, you play with meanings, you fabricate events, places . . . I know. It's all clever lies. And more power to

192

you for being able to carry it off. I'm just not very good at it. I just don't feel I could make something up and get away with it. Like I said; I'm too honest.'

'What does that make me then?'

'I don't know; how good's your writing?'

'Not very,' I said with a candour that surprised even me.

'Well, then you're probably not much of a liar. What can I say?'

I shrugged my shoulders. I had never thought of what I did as lying, and I wasn't completely sure I liked the idea, although in fact, the way David put it, he might well have had a case. But I was too tired to argue it out so I just laughed and nodded, and David laughed too, and any tension that might have existed in those few moments suddenly disappeared.

By the time I came to settle on the unlovely sofa in the common room I was aware that my mood had changed considerably since that morning; I was even feeling quite hopeful about my stay. At least I had stopped panicking for a short while. As far as I could tell, I had not been followed, and from what I had seen of the resort, with its remote location and air of decay, it seemed a good place to hang out for a while. Despite having told David my name, I could still be anonymous here, and that was the most important thing of all.

Consequently, I awoke this morning in a good mood to be greeted by smiling faces and bright sunshine. My sleep had been undisturbed by the dreadful nightmares that had plagued me, and for a moment or two I was almost able to forget my hellish predicament. Life, I mused, is perhaps not all bad.

Then again . . .

18

I read and re-read my photocopy of *The Fall of Man* over and over until I was so familiar with the contents that I felt I had written it myself. It is very difficult, I'm sure you'd agree, to be totally objective about any book in which you are the leading character, especially a book in which you are made to look pathetic and foolish, like a complete and utter prat. However, having distanced myself from the character of 'William' through these successive readings, I felt I had a clear understanding of Cassandra's thesis. If I had not, then there was no way I would have dared put my plan into action.

Oh yes, I had a plan. And it was brilliant. As I had suspected, Cassandra's typescript held the key to my salvation, the key that would unlock her hardened heart and, at one and the same time, prove my undying love and show me to be worthy of hers.

As it now stood, *The Fall of Man* was a dry, rather academic study that would, if and when published, find a pitifully small readership, most of whom would already be familiar with the territory; a clear case of preaching to the converted. If this was all that was to become of Cassandra's hard work, then (to my unstable and swiftly degenerating mind) it would be a tragic state of affairs, because what Cassandra had to say about the sex war was of *crucial* importance to everyone, men and women alike. For it to end up as some limited edition university text, bypassing the Great British Public, was nothing short of criminal. Alas, left to its own devices, there was no way it would attract anything more than nodding recognition.

But let us examine, for a moment, the elements that made up Cassandra's study; there was deception, the laying of a trap, insidious manipulation and the sort of graphic sex that would probably be censored if filmed. It was, in essence, very juicy material which, alas, due to Cassandra's necessarily scholarly style had had all the juice squeezed out of it. Even the sex scenes read like business reports. But with a bit of careful tweaking, a splash of sensationalism, spicing up the sex scenes and beefing up the fights and outrage, it could become the ultimate real-life thriller-romance. Will the brilliant, beautiful, sensual nineties woman succeed in her experiment and be hailed as a great pioneer? How will the poor, lowly struggling writer escape from the duplicitous trap that he's caught in? Will it end in disaster? Or will true love prevail?

In fact, all the classic ingredients of a massive bestseller!

With Cassandra's book I had found the solution to all my problems. Writer's Block would be a thing of the past; after all, the basic material was all here so there would be no fear of drying up or losing my way. And I knew it would be a success, both critically and financially. The highly acclaimed Meisterwerk that I had longed for was now within my grasp; it was just a matter of application. With *The Fall of Man* I had found my pot of gold, and there was no doubt in my mind that it was going to pay dividends.

Now before you all cry 'thief!', let me explain how I saw the situation. The original typescript had been written by Cassandra, and therefore you would be right in saying that it was her property and that she held the exclusive rights to the material. If I were to take the material as it stood and perpetrate some sort of 'passing-off' manoeuvre, then you would be well within your rights to accuse me of theft and fraud. But I was not stealing the material; I was borrowing it. The new book would be an original work *based* upon Cassandra's material. Without her knowledge. Okay, so maybe this doesn't entirely vindicate me, but remember, who was the source of all her material? It was me. And without me, there'd be no *The Fall of Man*. And as far as I was concerned, that gave me every right in the world to proceed with my plan. Besides, there's no copyright on ideas. Really. I looked it up.

Anyway, what's the big fuss about? I was doing it for *her*, wasn't I?

From the start I was aware that there were a number of difficulties with this project that would have to be dealt with in due course. Firstly there was the practical business of working on the 'revised edition' without letting on to Cassandra. This meant that I would have to work during the day while she was out. There was no question of writing in the evenings or attempting any late night sessions when she was in the house. Secondly, I would have to find a much more secure hiding place for my manuscript than Cassandra had for hers. If she were to stumble upon it before its completion, that would blow everything. Thirdly, I would have to find a way of presenting the idea to Cassandra in such a way that she would see immediately what a brilliant scheme it was. It would be all too easy for her to jump to the wrong conclusions; timing was crucial. If I waited until the manuscript had been accepted for publication, then Cassandra might think I really had stolen her book. However, until I had a guaranteed deal, there was the danger that Cassandra would veto its publication. In the end I figured that, as long as I signed over all the royalties to her, then there could be no objections. After all, I wanted nothing more than recognition for my efforts.

It seems inconceivable now that I could have been serious about this endeavour, that I could not see the flaws in my plan, the absurdities of even attempting to carry out this totally misguided labour of love. As it was, I took the whole exercise very seriously, dealt with the minutiae and technicalities carefully, without ever once confronting the essential dishonesty of the project. Could I not see that this was a recipe for disaster? That, far from being pleased with my noble attempt to bring Cassandra's hard work to the masses, she would consider my actions gross, outrageous, even criminal? Who the fuck was I to take her work and re-write it without her consent?

It is easy to see all this now, but back then, in my highly confused state, deranged and approaching dementia, it seemed the perfect answer. Cassandra would become rich and famous beyond her wildest expectations, and it would all be down to me. I would rise immeasurably in her estimations; she would see me for what I really was, a kind, loving, understanding man, cured of sexism, the very model of a New Man . . . and we would both live happily ever after.

Even if I was completely insane.

I started work on the re-write with more energy and enthusiasm than I had ever mustered for any other piece of writing. I worked with strict discipline and dedication from the moment the daily housework was finished until the moment Cassandra stepped through the doorway. I took no breaks for relaxation, food or drink, but worked steadily day in day out. The words flowed like a rushing stream (even if the contents more closely resembled a babbling brook). I was determined and unwavering. Anyone looking on would have said I was a man possessed.

And they would have been right.

Maxims and homilies are, by nature, anathema to me. However, if I have abided by any particular apothegm down the ages, it has been of the following order:

When life is tough, when the world is getting you down, when problems seem insurmountable . . .
. . . Run away.

It may be morally indefensible, but it is effective, and has held me in good stead for many years. I mention this here because, whilst technically I had had very little choice, it is pleasing to note that desertion still pays dividends.

After showering and dressing, I stacked my gear in the corner of the common room, sat down on the sofa, and waited for something to happen. Not that I had a right to expect anything good, anything pleasurable. But, well . . . hope springs eternal and all that.

One thing was certain though; I was surprisingly

hungry. Surprising, because after that first, dreadful evening when I had felt taunted by restaurants overflowing with beautiful people, I had lost interest in food altogether, and had been subsisting on whatever came to hand. But this morning I was indisputably ravenous. The mouth-watering odours of warm bread and freshly brewed coffee wafted into the common room from what appeared to be the kitchen, although whether this was a communal kitchen for guests or a 'staff-only' facility I didn't know.

I was just about to investigate when David walked in and sauntered over to where I sat. I greeted him with a smile; I recall it clearly, for the face muscles responsible for the action twinged slightly through lack of use. If David had known how rare that grin was he would have captured it and saved it for the nation.

'Hi Bill,' he said, his face glowing with that guilt-free vigour that comes only to those who have never truly sinned. Evidently, he didn't have a care in the world. 'Sleep well?'

For a moment my confident mood faltered; seeing him smiling and genuinely happy made me realise how false my own optimism really was; for a moment, as he stood there grinning at me, I was consumed with a deep, dark envy. But I tried not to show it.

'Surprisingly well,' I said, not wishing to feel bitter.

'That's good. Look, I've been told about this little café overlooking the sea that does a very reasonable breakfast. It's not far. How about we get out of here before it gets busy?'

I nodded approval. 'Sounds great.'

You see? If you hang around hopefully, and for long enough, something always happens.

Having grabbed the necessary minimum for a day's

lazing on the sand, David and I wandered out into the morning's brilliance. There was a strange, other-worldly quality to the atmosphere, not easily definable, that had been totally lacking from the north of the country. Whether it was just the quality of the light or something more organic, carried aloft by the sea breezes perhaps, I didn't know or much care. Whatever it was, it was wonderful, and brought about a sort of lazy, calming sensation that was quite irresistible. I breathed in this mystical ether with great and grateful pleasure.

'It's gonna be a beautiful day,' said David with rather more gravity than one might have expected, simultaneously pre-empting me of the only thought in my head. Perhaps here, with the sun beating down and the air full of drowsy delight . . . perhaps here I could just *forget* for a while.

'I'm really looking forward to just stretching out in this and soaking it all up,' I said, gazing around me with a peculiar and unwarranted contentedness.

'You look like you could use it. How long were you up north?'

'Just a week; it was depressing. All those pretty boys and girls on package tours. I couldn't stand it.'

'There's not too much of that down here; the tour companies have yet to discover this place. We should have the beach just about to ourselves. You'll be able to relax; the sun will lighten your load and your problems will all disappear. Take it from me.'

I smiled. Nothing could really lighten my load, I wanted to say, but didn't want to spoil the mood.

We made our way along the main road, past the small, local airport with its dusty runways and dilapidated buildings, and from there down to the beach. Cool pockets of air from off the sea teased the litter –

sheets of ageing newspaper and chocolate-bar wrappers – from out of the gutter and, whipping them up into little frenzies of activity, made them dance purposelessly along the pavement. A single gull glided effortlessly above us in the cloudless sky, round and round in ever decreasing circles, letting out an occasional anguished shriek before diving away out of sight.

After about ten minutes we rounded a corner and saw the platinum shimmer of early morning sun on water. The sea was calm and infused with a glorious aquamarine, and stretched out in uninterrupted glory to the horizon. The only café to be seen was situated on a rather makeshift wooden patio that led down onto the beach. There were three or four small round tables, a couple of 'Martini' parasols that had seen better days, and a slow, elderly waiter who clearly had not anticipated such early custom. We ordered coffee, bread rolls and honey and settled back in the rickety wooden chairs to admire the view. I was made suddenly aware of how long it had been since I had last gazed at the sea.

Cassandra and I travelled abroad together only once. It was inevitable, I suppose, that if I stayed with her long enough, eventually we'd go on holiday together, but I hadn't given the matter any thought. So it came as quite a surprise when, about a month or so after I had discovered the typescript, Cassandra suggested we take a break from the rat-race (or perhaps hamster race would be more appropriate, rats being few and far between in Hampstead).

Things between Cassandra and I had been rather quiet. My re-write of *The Fall of Man* was, by that stage, well advanced, and as I watched the pages mount up I became invigorated with a great sense of achievement.

Writing again – fluently, even joyously – was not only very satisfying in itself, it was also doing great things for my otherwise broken self-esteem. In fact, I was starting to feel vaguely human again. I got the impression that even Cassandra noticed this, although I don't think she much liked it. Instead of haranguing me for being miserable, she now chided me for being so damned cheerful. Didn't I realise that the last thing she wanted was to come home to some chirpy cockney sparrow who doesn't stop wittering on about how marvellous everything is?

You'd have thought by now that I'd have learned that there was no way I'd win where Cassandra was concerned. Still, I didn't let it upset me too much; there were more important things to hand, most particularly the *magnum opus* which was now taking shape and which, upon its completion, was guaranteed to win the affections of my beloved Cassandra.

So when Cassandra came home one evening complaining of fatigue and insisting we take a break, it threw me into momentary confusion. Whilst I had never been one to turn down an all-expenses paid holiday, I wasn't too keen on stopping writing now that I was in full flow. On the other hand, I had in fact used up the majority of Cassandra's material to date, and would shortly be reaching a temporary impasse. I mulled this over swiftly whilst Cassandra continued bemoaning her lot and telling me how exhausted she was. Perhaps a break would be good. We could go away for a while, relax, and then on our return, I could revise the work-in-progress whilst Cassandra got down to the job of churning out new material. Yes, a holiday would be good.

The following day Cassandra arrived home with armfuls of glossy holiday brochures, and requested that I help her look for something suitable. After much perusal, and having taken scant notice of either my recommendations or personal preferences, Cassandra settled for a week's half-board at a five-star hotel in Tangier. The package was remarkably cheap – too cheap – and although it had nothing to do with me (as I wasn't paying) I did my best to warn Cassandra that this might bode ill. For, in my limited experience, when it came to package tours, you got exactly what you paid for, which in this instance meant three o'clock-in-the-morning charter flights, half-a-dozen surcharges listed in suspiciously small print and a hotel that went by the unlikely (and I thought rather dubious) name of The Moroccan Fez. But try as I might to caution her, Cassandra was having none of it, insisting that the deal was exceptional value, and inexpensive only because this was an off-peak, last-minute booking. She chided me severely for my interference, made a number of comments concerning the fact that she was treating me to a holiday and you'd have thought I'd be grateful et cetera, and then accused me of not wanting to go to Tangier because I was unadventurous. Only then did it occur to me that, what with her flashy car, posh house and extravagant taste, Cassandra might have been overextending herself. Personally, I think she merely took exception to my use of the term 'dodgy' in tandem with something she had chosen to do.

So, realising once again that anything I thought or said counted for nought, and despite rather liking the idea of a holiday, I simply crossed my fingers and prayed that the Moroccan air-traffic controllers – long overdue, surely, in taking industrial action of any kind – would take it upon themselves to prevent the impending catastrophe by going on strike. Alas my prayers went unanswered and one week later, with Hope, Crosby and Lamour's lamentable theme tune humming incessantly in my ears, we were off on the road to Morocco.

The flight to Tangier was delayed by three hours. There's not much to do at Gatwick airport at three in the morning when you're tired and fatigued, and what there *is* is unlikely to keep anyone with even a modicum of curiosity satisfied for longer than half an hour. The time dragged slowly and, if one looked carefully, one could actually see Cassandra getting more and more riled by the minute; it was like watching the mercury in a thermometer rise, and flinching at the thought that, at any moment, it could explode off the end of the scale. When we finally took off we were greeted with freak weather conditions that caused so much turbulence that the stewardesses were unable to serve refreshments for two hours. This did little to moderate Cassandra's aggravated mood, and I became quite concerned for one of the poor stewardesses who, having no control over the circumstances, none the less had to bear the brunt of Cassandra's anger.

When, having suffered further delays at the arrival airport, we were finally shepherded to Tangier, my suspicions proved all too prescient. It is to be noted that there is no recognised international classification system regarding hotel accommodation, and it does not take a great imagination or indeed especial intelligence to predict that a Moroccan five-star establishment is in no way equivalent to its European or American counterpart.

The hotel foyer looked like a refugee camp, with what appeared to be several dozen homeless locals lounging about on the floor in various states of distress. It was only later that we realised most of these people were in fact hotel staff of one kind or another, many of whom lived so far from the hotel that it was less trouble to kip down in the foyer between shifts than go home for the night.

As for our room, it did, as promised, have a view and a balcony. Unfortunately the French windows that gave onto the balcony had been locked, bolted and nailed shut. We discovered later that this was due to an unfortunate accident the previous year concerning a large German chap who, tucking into his third shish kebab one evening whilst admiring the sunset, had plunged to his death when part of the balcony collapsed beneath him.

As for the view, we could indeed see the sea, as stated in the brochure. We could also see the hotel garbage dump, the electricity power station and what looked to me like Tangier's red-light district located, for convenience, no more than a hundred yards from the hotel's front entrance.

The bathroom had all the mod cons one might expect, plus a few others (lizards, cockroaches and percussive plumbing that, for some reason, vibrated with its greatest fervour at around two o'clock each morning) that one had not anticipated but for which, it must be said, no additional charge was made.

Still, it was not the end of the world. Until, that is, Cassandra got started. Undeterred, she did her level best to transform a potentially restful (if not especially luxurious) holiday into a total nightmare. It wasn't that Cassandra *liked* to complain about absolutely everything; I don't think there existed that degree of choice. Cassandra, you see, felt *obliged* to register her dissatisfaction at every possible moment. I believe it had something to do with existential angst. Upsetting menials, causing disruption and raising her voice gave Cassandra a greater sense of self. In a complex and confusing world, making a scene made her feel more *real*.

I think we were just unlucky as regards the weather, which is perhaps just as well as Cassandra was not inclined to venture across the railway tracks to test the waters. Or lie on the huge expanse of grey (yes, grey) sand which stretched like an industrial wasteland the entire length of the coast or, at least, as far as we could see.

'This is filthy!' said Cassandra, approximately five times a day, about anything and everything. Over the course of a week, this epithet was applied to The Moroccan Fez, its bedrooms, bathrooms, bars, restaurant and foyer. Equally it pertained to Tangier, its cafés, shops, merchants or just the city in general. Several times it was meant as an all-encompassing adjective to describe Morocco, its customs, weather and population at large. Tours were 'a rip off', shopkeepers 'thieving Arabs', hotel staff 'useless half-wits' and beggars 'disgraceful'. As usual I was merely 'pathetic' and consequently, when measured alongside the locals, I shone as a star in the firmament. It was the only time I was ever made to feel valued.

We didn't do very much with our seven days; by the time Cassandra had finished complaining there wasn't much time left for anything as specific as sightseeing. We wandered around the old parts of Tangier a few times, made a few valiant attempts at sunbathing – very much a hit and miss affair as, at any one time, you could guarantee that there would be more cloud than blue sky – and otherwise spent our time eating, drinking and sleeping. In fact, I'd never seen Cassandra sleep so much; I figured she must have been worn out from all that grousing and grumbling.

You may think that the trip, therefore, was nothing more than a miserable interlude in a life already comprising continuous despair. And, I suppose by and large, that's what it was. However there was one incident – one very revealing incident – that perhaps made the whole trip worthwhile.

On our final evening, having thoroughly exhausted Tangier's sparse attractions, we settled ourselves in the flashier of the hotel's two bars in order to down a few celebratory drinks before retiring for another early night. As we had booked our holiday out of season the hotel had been half-empty for the most part, and save for the occasional displaced Yank we had had the run of the place pretty much to ourselves. On that evening, however, we met with a young English couple who, like us, had taken advantage of the cheap deal. Unlike us, they had utilised their time in Morocco to great effect with numerous outings, excursions, coach trips, shopping expeditions ... all manner of activity, none of which we'd indulged in ourselves. This was probably why we hadn't seen them until that evening; they'd hardly spent any time in the hotel at all.

This young couple – Sue and Mike, I think it was – had had a splendid time. They'd found Tangier fascinating, Morocco exotic and even thought the hotel luxurious in a 'run down, olde worlde sort of way'. I believe their reaction to Morocco had a great deal to do with expectations or, in their particular case, lack of them. They had come on the spur of the moment with a great deal of enthusiasm and energy, and had had themselves a time to remember.

Whatever, the enthusiasm of this otherwise harmless couple did nothing to cheer up Cassandra, who had been in a particularly foul mood that day. On the contrary, having listened to Sue and Mike eulogise about their holiday, Cassandra lapsed into a dreadful depression which she attempted to camouflage with a false, forced jollity. In order to maintain a semblance of conviviality (and vent her continually distended spleen) Cassandra started to regale her captive audience with an extended and detailed catalogue of the disasters that had beset us since we'd arrived, embellishing each event with wild hyperbole and exaggeration, much to the amusement of our new acquaintances. Sue and Mike, unaware that Cassandra's garrulousness stemmed not from sociability but from a deep and bitter displeasure, entered into this quagmire of ill-feelings and theatricality with gay abandon, and plied us both with drinks for several hours, egging Cassandra on at every turn. By ten o'clock, Cassandra had forgotten herself and was ordering rounds of doubles.

We all got rather drunk, I perhaps less so than the others, since I had learnt to be always on my guard with Cassandra. I felt particularly nervous that night as, in all the time I had spent with her, I had never seen her in such a strange mood, and I sensed that it was in my interest to remain alert. Somewhere along the line there'd be hell to pay and I suspected that it would be me, albeit metaphorically, who would be picking up the tab.

At about midnight, Mike and Susan – thoroughly sloshed and still giggling like a couple of kids – made their excuses and staggered off to their room. Cassandra bade them a loud and rather hysterical goodnight whilst I braced myself for whatever onslaught was forthcoming. Although she was being particularly loud, she had not yet turned aggressive and, having finished the last of her drink, she agreed without fuss that it was time to go to bed. Alas, this was easier said than done, as Cassandra – who had probably consumed the best part of a bottle of gin – was all over the place, and it was all I could do to keep her upright as we mounted the stairs.

Once in the bedroom, and still making one hell of a racket, Cassandra collapsed on the bed and, slurring to the point of incomprehension, ordered me to turn off the light and take my trousers down. Although I was feeling considerably less than amorous at that precise moment, like a good boy I did as I was commanded, falling over several times in the process. Clearly I had drunk more than I realised.

I helped Cassandra out of her clothes and then fell on-to the bed beside her. She was still rambling like an idiot and muttering something about wanting a really decent fuck for a change. She then changed tack and started in on a lengthy and fanciful exposition concerning the probable length of Mike's dong. She tried taunting me with this for a while, perhaps in the hope of bringing me to life but, unfortunately, thanks to a combination of alcohol, fatigue and the usual fear, nothing short of a block and tackle would have readied me for action.

For a moment or two, fearing the worst, I did my best to distract her attention from my own shortcomings with a few rough fumblings in the dark. This didn't seem to do anything for Cassandra, and I had all but resigned myself to another slagging off when I realised that Cassandra had stopped talking. I put my head closer to hers, but all I could hear was an odd, muffled sound as she muttered rather desperately into the pillow. Fearing that she might be suffocating, I turned away and reached for the bedside lamp, but Cassandra reached round and pulled me back. She buried her face, already wet with tears, into my chest and started sobbing.

Cassandra crying? I was so shocked that all I could do was lie there, silently, and try to comfort her in my embrace.

I figured that she was just overly emotional from the drink and exhaustion, and even as I comforted her I half-expected her to suddenly spring to life and start hitting me. But Cassandra made no attempt to move and just lay there, weeping rather pathetically. I waited anxiously; this was something completely new to me and, as always in these situations, I feared the worst.

After a minute or so I suddenly felt her hand stroke my cheek, very gently; her fingers were damp and they trembled as she touched my skin. This in itself was completely out of character, and just as I was trying to adjust to this strange caress, the most surprising thing of all occurred. She pulled her face away from my chest, swallowed noisily and sniffed.

'I wish it wasn't you,' she said softly through her tears. 'I wish to God I wasn't doing this to you.' And then she fell silent.

Five minutes later she threw up all over the bed.

The coffee was hot and aromatic, easily the best I had had so far. David and I ate slowly, pleasurably, savouring the experience. The long, sandy beach was empty save for the shadows cast by the palm trees, located at strategic intervals along the strand. The only sounds to be heard were those of the sea lapping thirstily at the sand, and the breeze brushing through the palm leaves. And, of course, our relaxed chatter as we endeavoured, with notable sensitivity on David's part, to discover a little of each other's motives for being here.

With each exchange it became clear that David was an intelligent and gentle soul which, oddly, made talking to him all the more frustrating. Here was someone, I felt sure, who would understand; someone who would listen to my story and be able to empathise and comprehend all that had happened. But how could I even begin to tell him the truth?

An hour passed slowly. Time seemed precious and malleable, no longer tied to the constant tickings of watches and clocks. The sun began to rise to a more prominent position, and when the last of the coffee had been drained we paid the bill – inexpensive as David had promised – and dragged our towels across the sand to a semi-sheltered spot by the water beneath an isolated overhanging palm.

I positioned myself away from the tree, directly in the unobscured rays and allowed the raw heat to irradiate my sun-shy body, penetrating one layer of suntan oil and several of dead skin, to bake my flesh to the bone.

A couple of hours passed. Tense muscles slackened and relaxed as an inner glow pulsed through me from top to toe. My thoughts – a knotted mass of worries, fears and uncertainties – began to untangle. Loosened and allowed to drift, all my problems seemed to dissipate into the ether. I was medium-rare when, spurred by an unconscious stimulus, I rose unsteadily to my feet, my vision blurred, and stumbled across the sand and dived into an icy heaven.

Blame it on the sun if you wish, or put it down to my advanced dementia, but I swear that what happened next is true. When I opened my eyes beneath the surface of the water, I was confronted by – God help me – a mermaid. She was swimming towards me from a distance of about thirty feet, and she was smiling.

And perhaps I would not have been half as shocked had she not looked so uncommonly like Cassandra.

19

I did not forget Morocco in a hurry.

Having rid herself of a week's wages worth of booze, Cassandra fell into a comatose state for the rest of the night, during which time she scared the shit out of me on two separate occasions by neglecting to breathe for what seemed like several minutes at a time. She woke, unsurprisingly, with a foul hangover and a worse temper. The journey home, instead of being merely a miserable conclusion to a lousy trip, was transformed into a trial by fire. I learned what hell was that day. I curled myself into a little ball and tried to pretend I didn't exist. It didn't work. I arrived home tired, tetchy and ready for a holiday. I didn't get one.

I never found out if Cassandra remembered what she had said that night. Needless to say, she never mentioned it, and I was smart enough not to bring up the subject either then or at any time thereafter. However, in the aftermath, I had not been left untouched by Cassandra's drunken and weepy confession. One could not but admire Cassandra for her dedication. Despite her doubts concerning the morality of what she was doing, even at this late date (at least, that was how I had interpreted her disclosure) she was still prepared to see it through to the end. Amazing. If she did indeed feel, in her heart of hearts, either guilty or sorry for what she had put me through, then was it not astonishing that only under the influence of excess alcohol and extreme stress did she fracture and let a little anguish hiss out through the tiny rupture in her emotional armour plating? Like I said; admirable.

Not that it made any difference in the long run; she still treated me like shit. But somehow it didn't hurt so much now. For a moment, albeit briefly, I had seen the truth, a truth that I had not believed existed. Cassandra cared; she cared for her sorry little clown.

There was one question, however, which did arise following our trip, a question that started to play on my mind more frequently and with greater urgency once we had returned from Morocco: how long was she prepared to continue with her ground-breaking study? I had already noted that telling sentence in her typescript following my little ruse, that 'as predicted, *about half-way through the study*, William began to develop and execute certain skills . . .' Oh yes, I was well aware that the clock was ticking away and that I had only a limited time to complete my revision of her book. However, whilst Cassandra was still writing it, I felt safe.

Unfortunately, for several weeks following our holiday, Cassandra's typescript remained moribund. Every morning, after she had set off to work, I would check the bottom drawer, and every morning I was greeted by the same sight. The script had not been touched. There was no way of knowing whether she was still writing and keeping the additions to the typescript at work, or had stopped writing altogether. As the weeks wore on, whilst wishing fervently for the former, I secretly suspected the latter. Although Cassandra's behaviour did not differ greatly from before, she was no

213

longer 'working late' as often (I had long realised this was when Cassandra wrote her manuscript). This was very worrying. If Cassandra had merely slowed her output and was keeping the new material at work, then how would I finish the book? And if she had given up completely . . . well, it did not bear contemplating.

All the while I kept hope alive by assuming that, if the experiment were at a premature end, I would already have been given my marching orders. In their absence, I resigned myself to the possibility that the book had merely stalled and would not be finished for some time, and set myself to polishing what I already had.

But that wasn't the end of my worries. We had been home only a couple of weeks when Cassandra began exhibiting a certain listlessness that I'd never seen before. As it was so unlike her to be lethargic or indifferent about anything, I figured that she must be suffering from some nutritional deficiency. I didn't dare mention to Cassandra that she was looking under the weather, as I knew what I'd receive for my impertinence. So, rather than make a fuss or cause a scene, I took it upon myself to make suitable amendments to her diet, and hoped that it would make a difference. It did. On the third night of the new dietary regime, Cassandra took one look at the freshly prepared high fibre salad and hurled her plate at me, explaining in unambiguous terms that she was categorically *not* a fucking bunny rabbit. And if I insisted on feeding her nothing but lettuce leaves and raw carrots then before long she would start leaping about the house, twitching her nose and shitting on the carpet.

I was pleased to see a flash of the old Cassandra vitriol again, even if there was no subsequent upturn in her general levels of interest and activity. But the diet reverted to normal; I cared for Cassandra's health but I wasn't prepared to shed blood for it.

Still, I didn't feel wholly comfortable about this latest turn of events. Despite the fact that I remained the proud owner of an impressive collection of Pavlovian responses that virtually dictated my every move, I was none the less aware of a slight slackening of the rope that had become a permanent fixture about my neck. To begin with, I put it down to fatigue on her part; it must be exhausting being a full-time tyrant.

However, as the weeks began to slip by, and as Cassandra showed continuing signs of apathy, one thought continued to play on my mind. What if Cassandra, for some reason, was calling a halt to the experiment prior to its conclusion and was, consequently, in the process of finding some way of getting rid of me? Or what if it had already finished without me knowing, and she was merely waiting for an opportunity to tell me?

It was an awful, sickening idea, but one which was never far from my thoughts. I began to dwell on it more and more. What if, one day, she came home from work and just told me to piss off? Until Morocco I hadn't even considered the prospect of living without Cassandra, but the more I thought about it, the more possible – even likely – the scenario became. After all, she must have put a time-limit on the study; it couldn't continue indefinitely.

That was it. I became preoccupied with the thought that Cassandra was planning to get rid of me. It began to affect my concentration; I soon found myself unable to write for more than five minutes without becoming distracted. I started losing sleep. What started off as mere concern soon turned to real anxiety, and then to fully fledged fear.

And then to anger.

How could she? How *dare* she? She had swept me off the streets, severed my connections, pumped me full of the Hampstead good life (ha bloody ha), turned me into little more than a pet, a Cassandra-junkie. And now, without a second thought or 'by-your-leave', she was just going to open the door and kick me out onto the streets to fend for myself. And what existed to stop her? Her conscience? Ha! After all, as had been established long ago, Cassandra didn't really care for me at all, not really; a few drunken tears in a foreign hotel room didn't count for much when measured against the months of belittling and abuse I had endured. It was time to face facts; I was just a subject in her experiment, and if the experiment had run its course, then it was just a matter of time before my services would no longer be required. I was, ultimately, dispensable, and of no more use to her than an empty packet of washing powder. I was all used up.

And what of my master plan, to re-write her book and win her back? It would all have been for nothing. After everything I'd been through, after everything I'd suffered! It was despicable that she could even consider such a thing. Was she completely heartless? She couldn't do it to me. It wasn't fair, it wasn't right. She just couldn't do such a thing . . .

But of course by then I knew damn well that she was not only capable of it, but could carry it through with impunity, without hesitation, and with not a trace of conscience.

The *bitch*.

And how do you suppose that would affect me, eh? I'll tell you, shall I? I'd be fucked. Understand? Totally and completely fucked. Fucked fucked fucked. Fucked

fucked fucked fucked fucked. Fucked fucked fucked fucked fucked fucked fucked fucked fucked fucked fucked fucked . . .

'She did?'

'Uh-huh.'

'Incredible,' said David, sitting forward in his chair and smiling at me. 'So what happened next? Come on, come on . . . tell me!'

The sun had just descended into the sea in a riot of flame and fire, setting light to the blue and purple sky before clutching it and dragging it beneath the water in an explosion of red and golden glory. It was, quite simply, the greatest sunset I had ever seen.

We were still at the beach enjoying a couple of cold beers beneath the parasols. Very few people had followed us to this remote little spot and as David had predicted, we'd had the place pretty much to ourselves for most of the day. A half dozen people had now gathered to watch the sun go down – a daily ritual from what I could make out – but no one bothered anyone else, happy to involve themselves with the spectacle as if it were a specifically individual activity, a meeting with nature's more flamboyant displays, a communion.

'No, I think that's all for today.'

'What! Are you crazy? You can't do this! I have to hear more.'

'Yes, well, like I said; tomorrow.'

I don't know what prompted me to start telling David my story. Perhaps it was that extraordinary vision that I'd had after diving into the water. Or perhaps it was just this need, this burning need to confess. Whatever, once I had started telling David about Cassandra I found I could not stop. We had spent almost the entire afternoon lazing in the sun side by side, me talking, David listening assiduously, egging me on. The story unfolded easily, and with each word came an infinitesimal yet perceptible sense of relief so that by the time the sun had gone down, despite being tired from all the talking, I felt curiously light-headed, almost drunk on my confession.

David gave a sigh and sat back in his seat. 'I don't know how you can do this to me; just when it's getting to the juicy bit.'

'I thought there'd already been plenty of juicy bits; if I'd known that's all you were interested in . . .'

'No no, you've got me wrong. I mean, the whole set-up is fascinating. Especially the dominance thing. I mean, what do you think that was all about? I mean, what were the limits? Did she ever beat up on you?'

'David, please,' I said with a touch of disapproval, not because I thought David was talking out of turn, but simply because I didn't want to discuss it. I was happy to tell him the story, at my pace, in my own good time. But I didn't want to be questioned.

'Oh come *on*; this is no time to get coy. I'm genuinely interested.'

'I'll bet.'

'What, you think I'm a dirty old man or something like that?'

'Something like that.' I smiled, but I don't think David saw me.

He paused a moment, clearly considering his position. 'Well, yeah, I can see how you might think that. But believe me, it isn't the dirty stuff I really want to hear.'

'No? Then what?'

David drew in a deep breath and looked down at his feet; he seemed strangely embarrassed. 'It's her. It's

218

Cassandra. I want to hear more about Cassandra. You must understand? I need to know *everything* about her . . .'

See what I mean? He hadn't even laid eyes on her and already he was obsessed, desperate for information, an addict, a Cassandra-junkie, just like me, just like Cassandra's little clown.

Poor sod.

20

Well, was someone following us back from the beach last night or not? And if they weren't following us, what *were* they up to? People don't behave like that unless they've got something to hide. Take it from me. Take it from someone who knows. Say what you like, but *I* know there's something going on here. I didn't say anything about it to David; David and I have become really close these last couple of days, and I don't want anything to drive a wedge between us. I *need* him now; I need him to hear me out, to listen to the end of my story, to hear my terrible confession. I don't want him thinking I'm just some nutter with a highly developed sense of paranoia. Even if that's the truth.

But it isn't like that. It isn't paranoia. I tell you, I *know* something's going on. Like Dai, that Welsh git who runs the hostel. Oh yes, he's all smiles and *bonhomie* when I first arrive, but where's the good will now, where's the 'hail fellow well met' now? I'll tell you where. It's crawling around the floor like a fucking cripple, having been beaten out of him by those two goons *WHO ARE FUCKING FOLLOWING ME!* Yep, someone got to Taffy, and now instead of inquiring if I've had a nice day, he's asking personal, intrusive questions like where am I from and what do I do and when did I leave home and I'll tell you something straight, he doesn't fool me for one moment, not one fucking moment. Fuck the Welsh; you can't trust them, you really can't. Why do you suppose we still talk about 'welshing on a deal'? Think it's just a coincidence, do you, boyo?

It's a shame, it is. It's a real shame. Just as I was beginning to feel comfortable here. But it's no good, I'll have to move on. Fuck it; and I was starting to feel *so* good.

We headed back to the café on the beach. The sun was bright, the sea was glistening like one giant, liquid jewel, but I didn't feel good. Not only was I upset about last night, about being followed and about that nosey Welsh bastard, but today David is really pushy. I can't blame him; he wants to hear the end of the story.

'So, what happened next?'

'Okay, okay, relax will you.'

'Impossible. I already told you, I *have* to know more. You can't tell me you're surprised.'

I shook my head, perhaps a little wearily. 'No, I suppose not. She had that effect on everyone.'

David looked at me searchingly. 'Had?' he said, clearly suspicious. He didn't take his eyes off me, and I could see he was weighing something up, working something out. I felt uncomfortable beneath his glance. 'Actually,' he said after what seemed like an eternity, 'that's another thing that's been puzzling me. Cassandra. Sometimes you talk about her in the past tense, sometimes in the present. Sometimes it's 'Cassandra does this', sometimes 'Cassandra did this' . . . that's very strange, you know that?'

Oh yes, I did know that. I knew very well. I attempted

to make good this lapse as swiftly as possible but I faltered, fumbling for words and falling over my own tongue. 'I guess . . . I just haven't accepted that it's over . . . part of me wishes . . . I wish it was still there, that it still existed . . . the relationship . . .' I ran out of steam. I looked up at David, but I could see he didn't believe a word.

There was another long silence. I drained my coffee cup and beckoned to the waiter for a refill. I felt hot and sweaty even though we were sitting in the shade. It wasn't supposed to be like this, it wasn't supposed to be an interrogation. I just wanted to tell David the whole story without being questioned . . .

'Something happened, didn't it?' he said suddenly, grabbing my wrist harshly as if I might leap up and run away. 'Something bad happened.'

I tried to wrest myself free of David's grasp, but he was strong and held on tightly. 'What are you talking about? Let go David; you're making me uncomfortable.'

But David did not let go. He leant closer. He took a deep breath and lowered his voice to a whisper.

'What happened, Bill?'

What happened indeed. David has been listening carefully to my woeful tale. He is intelligent enough to realise that something in my story isn't quite right, that something isn't sitting easily in this web of deceit and despair, that I am deliberately misleading him in some sense. Has he guessed, I wonder?

Have you?

I sit there silently for a few moments, squirming under David's interrogative glare. This need to 'spill the beans', to tell all, rises up in me once again. How much longer can I keep it to myself? I look around the empty beach café. It's surely just a matter of time until they move in and get me – I know this now. I've been fooling myself too long. And when they come, it'll all be over. There'll be no one to understand me then. And I desperately want someone to know what really happened.

I look down to where David's hand grips my wrist, and slowly he loosens his hold. But the pressure inside me has not abated, and like a volcano that's about to erupt, I feel an uneasy grumbling in the depths of my being and know that, one way or another, the truth will out.

So I tell him.

It was a Thursday evening. Cassandra came home at about seven in a foul mood. I fetched her G and T and asked about her day. But Cassandra did not respond. She didn't collapse onto the sofa in her usual manner either. Instead, she walked into the kitchen and stood by the sink, looking out through the window, her back turned towards me. I followed her but kept my distance. She looked agitated. All day I had been in a frantic state. My fears and concerns that the experiment was over had virtually overwhelmed me, and I had already guessed that, when the time came, it would all happen something like this. It would *not* be a normal day, Cassandra would *not* behave in a normal manner. And neither, I was sure, would I.

Now, as I watched her, I could see that there was something about the way she stood, about her uncompromising silence that rang alarm bells. Something was wrong; something was desperately wrong. I tried to control the panic, but I knew what was coming; I just knew. I waited patiently for Cassandra to say something, anything. My hands were trembling and my throat had become very dry. Cassandra said nothing. The tension in the air was palpable; you could almost see it, this thick, black, rubbery band that connected us stretched almost to its limit. I felt sick. The silence was pressing down on me, crushing me.

'What is it?' I croaked.

Cassandra did not respond. My hands began to shake.

'Tell me what's wrong? Is there something wrong? Is there?' My voice sounded feeble, on the edge of tears, yet every word was like a piece of broken glass in my throat.

Her shoulders heaved theatrically. 'William, I . . .' she began, then faltered. She turned, a look of anguish crushing those beautiful features, distorting her appearance like a trick mirror, so that for the first time she appeared old, even ugly. 'William, it has to stop.'

The bile rose in my throat. 'What do you mean?'

'Look, this isn't easy for me, so please don't make it any harder. I've come to a decision. I don't want you living here any more. I want you to leave.'

She had said it. The words, those words. Simple enough words; clear, precise, to the point. But not *ordinary* words. These were words that were chosen to hurt, words expressly selected to wound, to damage. 'I don't want you living here,' she said. 'I want you to leave,' she said. 'I hate you! I hate you! I hate you!' Not spoken, but resounding clearly between the lines.

I suddenly felt extremely light-headed, and my legs and stomach conspired between them to throw me off balance. I reached behind me and grabbed hold of the counter to steady myself. I had rehearsed a speech, a good speech, just for this moment, just for this event, but as I struggled to keep myself from slipping to the floor, I found myself dumb, unable to utter anything other than a barely audible moan.

'It's not open to discussion,' she continued, leaning back against the sink. 'Nothing you can say will change it. I've been thinking about it for a long time. This sounds like a dreadful cliché, but believe me William, it's for your own good. Please don't make a scene.'

It was incredible. Even now she was trying to be cool about it all, casting that blasted spell, that power she had over people. But even in my confusion and distress I could see she was having difficulty this time. She breathed in deeply a couple of times, and closed her eyes when she started to speak.

'Now listen to me carefully, William. I'm going away for a few days to give you a chance to make arrangements . . . obviously I can't expect you to leave tonight, but I shall be back on Tuesday, and when I return, I don't expect to find you here.'

'Where . . . where are you going?'

Cassandra frowned. She had clearly not expected me to inquire, no more than I had expected to ask.

'Well . . . Paris, if you must know.' She paused, summoning up that mythical strength that she always kept in reserve. 'It's the best thing. You'll just have to take my word for it.'

I wasn't surprised, of course not. But that didn't stop me from feeling like I'd been felled by a blow from out of the blue. I felt really sick now, like I might throw up all over the kitchen. My breaths were coming in sharp, staccato stabs and I had to fight to get the words out.

'You can't do this, Cassandra. Not now, not yet. You can't . . .'

'*Don't* . . . tell me what I can and can't do!' She yelled. She was evidently overwrought, trying desperately to keep control of the situation. 'I said I don't want a scene, and I mean it.' There was real anger in her voice now which she tried to suppress, but it wasn't working. Not just anger, either; there was hatred, loathing, disgust. You could see it oozing out of her like black slime. It was terrifying. 'You can keep the clothes, obviously, and I drew some money out for you. It's not much but it'll keep you afloat until you find somewhere to settle . . .'

'But you can't!' I screamed. 'What about us?'

'Stop it! There is no "us". It's over.'

But it wasn't over, it couldn't be. I still had to win her back; that's what I'd been planning all these months. She couldn't throw me out now, without giving me a chance to prove myself. She couldn't . . . it wasn't fair . . . there was no reason . . .

I was fading fast. I could see myself teetering on the edge of a black, bottomless pit of desolation; just one more push and that would be it. In desperation I played the only card left in my trembling hand.

'What about your fucking book!' I cried, anger and confusion taking hold of me in equal measure. 'What about *The Fall of Man*?'

That stopped her. She went quite pale and her eyes widened like a startled child. 'Jesus Christ!'

My legs were really shaking now; I tightened my grip on the counter. 'You can't send me away; it isn't finished yet . . .'

'What! What are you *talking* about . . .'

'The re-write . . . the book . . . just . . . just *listen* a minute. It's going to be brilliant, you'll be famous . . . the revised version, the one I've written. It'll be a bestseller . . . wait. Wait here.'

Summoning the final reserves of strength I dashed out of the kitchen, ran to the file I kept hidden amongst my papers, and came stumbling back with the typescript. I held the revised manuscript out towards Cassandra, whose expression was now an amalgam of shock and disbelief. The tears were cascading down my cheeks and I could hardly see. The pages of the script fluttered in my trembling hand like a wounded bird. 'See? Just look.'

Cassandra grabbed the script and began thumbing through it, shaking her head; I could see she was impressed. At least that's how it appeared through the tears.

'What on earth . . . ?' She looked up at me. 'For Christsake, what are you up to?'

'I wanted . . . I had to prove . . . Cassandra, I was doing it for you.'

'This is an outrage!'

That took me aback.

'No, please . . . I was just . . . you have to read it . . .'

'What *is* this?' she shouted. 'Why have you been doing this?'

She didn't look pleased about it. Not at all. I didn't understand. Surely she realised?

'Because . . . because I love you.'

And that was when her expression changed from disbelief to horror. I tried to convince myself that she was just surprised, a little shocked perhaps, but it didn't work. I knew what she was thinking; I could see it clearly in her eyes. Revulsion had contorted the lines of her face; less the ice-maiden, more the wicked witch. She hurled the script at me.

'How *dare* you!' she screamed. 'How *dare* you! Who the fuck do you think you are . . . my God, I don't believe it . . .'

'Don't Cassandra . . . please don't . . .'

'You stupid bloody ... you imbecile! What makes you think ... don't you know? You're just a hack, a worthless, talentless hack! You don't understand anything, do you?'

'Don't Cassandra ... you don't know what you're saying ...'

'Stop snivelling!' She started to move towards me, pointing accusingly and shrieking. I couldn't stand it. I backed away. 'Did you honestly expect to get away with this? What *can* you have been thinking? Are you *completely* mad?'

I backed into the counter and grabbed hold of it for support. I was dizzy and felt very ill. There was fire in her eyes now, not the sexy, passionate fire that I'd seen during the early days of our lovemaking, but a spiteful, angry fire that burned into me with undisguised hatred. I couldn't stand to look at her. I turned my back on her and leant heavily on the counter; my eyes were sore from the tears, and I could see nothing clearly any more.

But she wouldn't let me alone. She came up behind me, still cursing, and then started thumping her fists on my back.

'You idiot! You fucking idiot!' I could hear that she was crying, but I didn't care any more. I was hurting. I was hurting in a way that, even as it was happening, seemed inconceivable. My entire body felt ruptured, contused, as if every cell, every fibre, every bit of me was being beaten with hammers. With each blow of Cassandra's fists, a little more life was knocked out of me. And I had nothing to respond with; no energy, no will, nothing.

'I'm sorry,' I murmured. 'I made a mistake; I'm sorry ...' I didn't even mean it. I just wanted her to stop hitting me. I couldn't stand it. The blows were raining down on me now, each one infused with that disdain, that disgust that had probably always been there, always been at the heart of her actions, her feelings. I felt blackened and bruised, defeated. She started ranting like a madwoman.

I opened my eyes, but everything appeared blurred and nebulous. My world was losing all sense of solidity, of substance. And still she beat me with her clubbed fists. I was lost. I took a heavy blow in the kidneys and sank to my knees. As I fell, I was momentarily blinded by a bright flash. I flinched and turned my head away. But when my eyes had adjusted, I looked again and saw what had dazzled me. There it was, lying on the counter.

It was solid and real. Its finely-honed edge had caught the light, and it now glinted at me through the haze.

I reached out.

'Don't you know what I've been through?' she screamed, still laying into me with heavy punches. 'I've abandoned that fucking book *because* of you, because I couldn't bear it any longer! Don't you see? I'm letting you off the hook! Now get out of here!'

I didn't understand a thing she said. They were just words now. Not evil or hateful. Just meaningless words.

'Did you hear me? I want you out of this house, out of my life, out of the country! Go! Go, and don't come back until . . .'

The blade sliced her throat as easily, as effortlessly as if it had been an onion.

I left her there on the kitchen floor, the blood still pulsing from her throat. The money she had intended to give me was in her purse; just over three hundred pounds. I took it, packed my shoulder-bag, grabbed my passport and fled to the airport, where I took the first flight going anywhere. I figured no one would discover her for a few days. She would have told her boss, her work colleagues, and probably her friends that she was going to Paris for a long weekend; no one would be looking for her until Tuesday, perhaps Wednesday. Once discovered, the police would make their usual enquiries and once they'd narrowed down the suspects they'd be out searching for a Schmidt, Dr W., which was how every one of Cassandra's acquaintances knew me. Smith, Mr B., would therefore have a few days grace at least.

'Go,' she had said. 'And don't come back until . . .' Until what? Would she really have had me back? It doesn't bear thinking about. What on earth had she meant to say? Until you're better? Until I'm over this?

Until hell freezes over?

I guess I'll never know.

David gave a deep sigh. Then he smiled. 'Nice try,' he said.

I frowned. 'What do you mean?'

'You writers! Jesus, you really had me going there for a while. Shit. I tell you Bill, it's a great story. And it'll make a great book.' He punched me lightly on the shoulder. 'I reckon you're a much better writer than you've been making out.'

'But David . . .'

'Okay, I did my bit. I listened without questions. But now you gotta tell me the truth. Cassandra really exists, right? But what about the rest of it? Did any of that crazy stuff really happen?'

That's when I started laughing. I laughed uncontrollably, until the tears scored lines on my cheeks, until I was breathless, until I could barely stand it.

'What? What is it?' said David, his smile tainted with bemusement. 'What did I say?'

I shook my head, still struggling for breath. Out of the corner of my eye I saw two uniformed men enter the café and walk over to the waiter. One of the policemen took something from an inside pocket and showed it to the waiter who studied it for a moment and then pointed towards the table where David and I were sitting.

'Well?' said David. 'What did I say that was so funny?'

The two uniforms walked towards us.

'Nothing,' I wheezed. 'Nothing at all.'